THIRST

Also by A.G. Mojtabai

Mundome

The 400 Eels of Sigmund Freud

A Stopping Place

Autumn

*Blessed Assurance: At Home with the Bomb
in Amarillo, Texas*

Ordinary Time

Called Out

Soon: Tales from Hospice

All That Road Going

Parts of a World

Shine on Me

THIRST

A Novel

A. G. MOJTABAI

THIRST
A Novel

Slant
An Imprint of Wipf and Stock Publishers
199 W. 8th Ave., Suite 3
Eugene, OR 97401

www.wipfandstock.com

HARDCOVER ISBN: 978-1-7252-7481-5
PAPERBACK ISBN: 978-1-7252-7480-8
EBOOK ISBN: 978-1-7252-7482-2

Cataloguing-in-Publication data:

Names: Mojtabai, A.G. | Mojtabai, Grace | Mojtabai, Ann Grace
Title: Thirst : a novel /A.G. Mojtabai
Description: Eugene, OR: Slant, 2021.
Identifiers: ISBN 978-1-7252-7481-5 (hardcover) | ISBN 978-1-7252-7480-8 (paperback) | ISBN 978-1-7252-7482-2 (ebook)
Subjects: LCSH: 1. Catholics — Fiction. / 2. Death — Fiction / 3. Clergy — Fiction / I. Title
Classification: PS3563.O374 T45 2021 (print) | PS3563.O374 (ebook)

Manufactured in the U.S.A.   NOVEMBER 9, 2020

For Richard Giannone and Frank D'Andrea

O Lord who has set the sun in heaven but chosen to dwell in thick darkness.

—*I Kings* 8:12

Ich kenne dich, du bist die tief Gebeugte. . . .
I know you, you are the deeply bowed. . . .

—Paul Celan, *Breathturn into Timestead,*

translated by Pierre Joris

CONTENTS

I

MIDDAY

"IS THAT YOU, FATHER?" Sister Perpetua calls, speaking through the door. The door is unlocked but he waits for her to open it.

"Still blowing out there?" she asks.

"Off and on," he says.

"You're almost late—it's not like you, Father. Are you all right?"

"Fine. Better than I deserve," Father Theo says, his reply for all occasions. Aware he is being watched, he quickens his pace as he moves ahead to where the others are waiting.

Day after day, the same ragtag procession: First, the propped (Dorothy, Hildegard, Sixtus, Cecilia), in silence but for the clack of canes; then the walker on wheels (Dymphna); then the wheelchair (Josepha). Sister Perpetua follows, on her own, with unfaltering step, the only one.

They are—*count them*—all of the seven remaining, the eighth, Sister Martha, having gone to her eternal reward the week before. Father Theo files in after the sisters. He's been a frequent noontime guest since Father Nolan, their regular chaplain, assumed extra duties elsewhere. Father Theo is dragging now, as though trudging uphill.

All but Sister Perpetua have grown old in service here.

Tower bells herald the noon hour, proclaim an ordered world. The sisters chorus: "The angel of the Lord declared unto Mary. . . ." Those who are able to stand for the Angelus do so; kneeling is not an option.

They spread out loosely over the long table in the refectory as if to colonize the emptiness. The white oilcloth gleams, immaculate but for a frayed spot here and there where the shining surface has worn through, exposing the underweave.

So many vacant places. . .so many echoes! Once upon a time this hall was filled with young, clear voices, singing and laughter, for despite the name of their order "Servants of the Sorrowing Mother," also known (teasingly, among certain priests) as "the Sorrowful Sisters," they were a joyous bunch in their younger days. And they were spunky: "To the great I AM, say 'we are!'" was one of their shout-songs. They were nurses and teachers, living in the world and out of it, at a time when vocations were plentiful. Forty-some professed, a dozen or so in the various stages of postulancy and the novitiate, everything clicking right along—so different from this year when their one and only novice quit and gave no reason. As if the reason were all too obvious.

They sit, then bless themselves. Bean soup and cornbread today. Some sort of dessert—pudding— whitish. Father Theo dabbles in the soup, takes several bites of the cornbread, postpones the pudding.

Banners grace the four walls proclaiming *Morning with Jesus*, *Midday with Jesus*, *Evening with Jesus*, *Renewed by His Grace*. A portrait of the foundress, Mother Bernarda, is positioned midpoint between *Morning* and *Midday*. She is wimpled in the old habit, neck and ears under wrap. She seems to be smiling, but faintly, slightly off-center, as if losing patience. Year after year she's been put up for beatification, but she's not there yet, remaining merely "Venerable"—worthy of veneration, not yet "Blessed." And she'll need two miracles after "Blessed" to boost her up to "Saint." So far, one sister's claim to a miraculous cure has not been authenticated— in fact, the recipient (Sister Martha) is the one who has just died.

Father Theo finds himself sitting next to Sister Hildegard and across from Sister Cecelia. "I dreamed about you last night," Sister Hildegard ventures.

"Oh? Pleasant, I hope?"

"Strange. Very strange. You were leading a herd of white-faced cattle. You know the kind—their bodies and ears are black with white markings. They were grazing, moving across the field here, and some of them were straying. You started crossing the highway and never once looked back. What does it mean? You're not thinking of leaving us, are you?"

"How should I know?" he answers. "It was *your* dream, not mine."

"Do we own our dreams, I wonder?"

A flurry of speculation follows. Are dreams messages? Or mere detritus, sweep-ups of unfinished personal business from the day?

Meanwhile, Sister Cecelia has been bursting to get a word in. "Have you noticed how the days are warning?" she says. "But it's still too chilly to go outside and play."

Charity is called-for. It's not clear whether it's only her speech that's failing, or her hearing, or her mind, or possibly all three together. One must listen carefully: "We are swimmers—all" concerns "sinners." Friday becomes "flyday." Best not to argue or press for clarification. All signs point to the End of Time.

"Jesus is coming," Sister Cecelia concludes, "and that spells it all."

Father is leaving. Rising abruptly, he gathers his plates, nudging the pudding aside untouched. *Be quick!*—he feels the gimlet eye of Sister Sixtus upon him. "I saw you only pecking at your plate, Father. Don't carry the fasting too far," she scolds. He hurries his dishes to the sink, scrapes and stacks them, hoping for a clean getaway.

Which is not to be—for Sister Perpetua is close on his heels. She draws him out of the hallway and into the deserted Host Room. Neither makes a motion to close the door. Leaving the door open is scarcely necessary but old rules become second nature at last.

* * *

SINCE SISTER MARTHA'S PASSING, Sister Perpetua has been acting Superior of the convent. She's the youngest of the group, somewhere in her fifties, which is not so young, but looks apple-cheeked and positively farm-fresh in comparison with everyone else here. Feeling herself to be a generation apart sometimes, she needs to vent. It comes out in a burst:

"We still have open house, our day of discernment, as you know. Last year we baked a hundred cookies, and two girls showed up. We always hope, we never learn. Those who come are mostly curious to know what goes on here—they think of it as a secret place. So they think it's 'cool' to investigate. But no one is willing to commit or give it a serious try. Not one single aspirant. I guess you know what happened to our one and only novice?" but here Sister Perpetua breaks off. She has begun to weep. The girl's departure still rankles—a desertion and a harbinger of things to come.

They stand facing the idling press, like a giant waffle iron, jaws gaping, a statement in itself. Altar breads are no longer made here.

Father counsels the usual: "patience. . .tides turn. . .you never know. . . ."

Again, she brings up the smashed window in the chapel. That happened a year ago, and has long since been repaired, but clearly continues to haunt her. "Who would do such a thing?"

"Kids. . . ." Father shakes his head sadly, "kids!"

He passes through the hall with eyes on his feet, heedless of the many self-improving mottos in English, Spanish, and German, hand-lettered and framed, dotting the long corridor. He assumes that nothing new or startling has popped up between yesterday and today—or in however many months since he stopped noticing.

Before leaving, he pauses in the vestibule, though. He stands before the icon of Mary Undoer of Knots. It's an old Bavarian devotion and a great favorite of the sisters here. *Maria Knotenlöserin. . . . Take into your hands this knot.* A puzzling painting, he's always felt. . . . Mary stands, flanked by angels, serpent writhing underfoot. She is working away at a knotted rope or ribbon; cherubs play with the dangling ends. The problem is, the longer he stares at it, the less clear it becomes whether she's loosening the knots or creating new ones.

* * *

WEATHER ON THE WAY. . . . Clouds blot what little sun there was before Father Theo entered the convent at noon. He isn't properly dressed for the chill but knows that if he steps inside his house to fetch a jacket he'll be disinclined to face the outside again.

The day had not started well. One of those marriage-preparation sessions. He was only filling in for

Father Nolan and had never met the couple before—no surprise that he'd not connected. Once upon a time, he might have dismissed the episode as "just one of those situations that come with the territory," part of his job description, more or less routine. Nothing new. But even as a young priest he found he preferred funerals to weddings, and over the years he'd learned that he wasn't the only priest who felt this way. *Then* at least people were serious. He had no patience for the usual silliness at wedding rehearsals. And—funeral directors didn't take over, monkeying with the lights in the sanctuary, trying to create special effects, as wedding consultants loved to do. "I don't go to your house and mess with your lights," he'd scold them. But it wasn't his house, and there'd been too many funerals. . . .

And as for preparation and advice—realistically—what could a priest, a lifelong celibate, be expected to know about marriage? He's well aware that the young regard priests as either effectively neutered and without a clue, or repressed, simmering with envy and resentment—singularly unsuited to the task of marriage advisor, either way. And yet, and yet. . .as he kept on reminding himself, he did know *something*. Something about commitment.

He wasn't feeling well—he was exhausted, was all—that's how he explained it to himself afterwards. He wanted to help out Father Nolan, but it would have been kinder to everyone involved if he had begged off.

The couple in question was attractive enough. In their early twenties, wearing perfectly matched track suits. Before settling in, they scraped the linoleum, pushing their chairs up against one another so there'd be no separation between them, even momentarily. They were demonstrably "in love"—*it would not suffice*, he knew.

He'd asked them to turn off their smart phones and place them on top of his desk in hopes that they might, just possibly might, pay attention to what he had to say.

Vain hope! When they weren't gazing at one another they cast longing glances at their phones, never eyeing Father Theo directly.

All he knew about them were their names, ages, baptismal and confirmation dates. And the fact that both listed the same address—which told him they were living together.

Anger and impatience have been his besetting sins, he knew. If anything, these passions had grown worse as he aged. But over the years he'd learned to muffle his irritation to some extent. Tempted to say something cutting now—something like: "What do you plan on doing after you're married that you aren't doing already?"—he thought the better of it and checked himself. Instead, he asked: "What do you think wedding cake means?"

"*Means?*" A puzzled silence followed, the young man telegraphing with a smile and a wink to his fiancé: *Can you believe this!* To make matters worse, Father Theo cupped one ear dramatically, as if waiting in deafness for the answer to fly in. *Bad scene!* "What are we talking about?" the young man exclaimed, sounding beside himself. "What does it *mean?* Way too many calories?. . . Overpriced?. . ."

But the question, the asker, was dead serious. "Cutting the wedding cake together—what does that mean? Does it mean *anything* to you?" Nothing, apparently, so he persisted. "The meaning, the real meaning of wedding cake, cutting it together, your hand over her hand, holding the knife, making the first cut. . . ." The two stared at one another blankly; they were stumped.

"I'll tell you what it means! In one of the nursing homes I visit there's a woman in her eighties suffering from Alzheimer's whose husband comes in to feed her every day. She doesn't speak or greet him, ever. Doesn't recognize him as anyone she's ever known. They've been married for more than fifty years and she has no idea who he is or why he bothers. Rain or shine every day—think of it! *That's* what wedding cake means."

His vehemence surprised him, his own voice—an old man's frayed voice—higher-pitched than normal, cranky, hectoring. His eyes filled. His eyes often teared up these days, suddenly, and for no reason.

But how could he blame them? They were so young—kids, really. Old age was another country.

He should have begged off.

* * *

STACKED AGAINST THE neighboring convent—a veritable castle—Father Theo's cottage seems a mere hutch.

Yet it suits him; he fills its contours completely, while the sisters rattle around, lost in a maze of corridors and empty cells. Years ago he'd laid down a stone path between the buildings and planted the bordering trees. He has planted many a tree in his lifetime. A few years back, he switched over to flowers.

Then, when even flowers became too strenuous, he summoned the handyman, Felipe, to help with weeding and tending. He put in most of the plants himself, but Felipe and the hybridizing outfit he ordered from seem to have added here and there, some of them surprises.

He's been calling on Felipe more and more these days. He's never sure when he's asking too much, for Felipe never refuses. When he'd asked: "Will you see me into the ground when the time comes?" Felipe answered as though it were the most natural request in the world: "You know I will, Father."

There are no flowers now, of course. Only—stalks; stubble; briar, brittle with cold; chicken-wire netting blown down; his spring flowers in the grip of winter still, name-tagged and bedded down under layers of hay and mulch, awaiting resurrection. The name-plates are laminated (surviving all weathers so far), staked low to the bed: *Puff. . .Praise Song. . .Lamplighter. . .Sage. . .Sailing On. . . .*

So many sailing on. So many gone. The good sisters will return to the motherhouse; the convent vacated, then gutted. Sister Perpetua knows this. No longer a question of years, but months now. The building will have to be scrapped; asbestos removal would be too costly. And the convent with its honeycomb of fifty-some cells is too singular a structure to be adapted to other uses, let alone bring up to code.

Everything passing. . . . But seasons return and, with them, his garden. . . . *Red Sedum. . . Flaming Poppa . . . Beckoning Tiger . . . Sea Glass*—

Sea Glass is one of the newer hybrid varieties; he's had it for two seasons. Part tulip maybe? Same shape, like a chalice or hand-bell. . . .

Seeing it in bloom reminded him of his first visit to the ocean, after a landlocked childhood and years of confinement in seminary. Combing the beach for shells, he'd stumbled upon these curious fragments. He recognized them for what they were, bits and pieces of once-ordinary bottle glass, abraded by stones and the salt wash of years, but with edges gentled now, incandescent, a frosty radiance at their core. Ordinary glass, slipping back, grain by grain, to the sand from which it was formed, and yet for the time being—a durable *now* on the human scale—no common stuff, so richly changed.

A durable now. . . . When he longs for permanence, why not think of this?

Isn't it enough? Why isn't this enough?

The wind is stiffening.

Feather Down. . .Lifted Hands. . . .

He tastes parched earth, caliche, at the back of his throat. There's a muffled pounding in the air, a surge, then sudden ebb, more felt than heard. Locals call it "falling weather," rain, snow, or hail, *something*—anyone's guess—about to fall. *Something surely coming.* Birds overhead swerve and spill out of formation, beating wings stilled, trying to read the wind.

Then they, too, pass.

The day comes together in him.

He does not want to outlive himself. His garden will go on without him. Time to turn and head home. *Now.* His mind is made up, his steps steadier, surer than they've been in months. But he halts before his own door, staring at the latch. Anyone would think he's lost his key, although he needs no key. He always keeps his door unlocked.

Now. It's time to head for cover.

Listen: the rattle of bare stalks, a shuffle of wings. *It's time.*

He enters his house. He will not leave it again.

2

LENA, HERE

IN DENVER FOR HER scheduled layover and con-
necting flight, she'd run into an unexpected glitch—a
blizzard, full-blown, out of nowhere. In minutes, the
stalled aircraft were blanketed with snow, their wings
webbed with drift. There were no runways; nothing
moved. One imagined a great hush-cloth draped over
everything.

*How strange to think it was already well into March,
so close to Spring.* Lena stood at the big window. The
scene was quite beautiful once you gave into the storm
and realized how lucky you were to be inside and on
firm ground, not airborne.

But after the first hour, when it became clear
that this was to be no brief intermission, passengers'
patience began to fray. Planes would be backed up for
hours; no officials would say for how long.

To add to this "inconvenience", the airlines were
short of meal and hotel vouchers. After arguing, and

getting nowhere, most of the stalled passengers re-signed themselves to trying to nap on the hard chairs, or the uncarpeted floor, or playing solitaire on their smart phones, making the best of a bad deal however they could. Only a few stood fast, planting themselves in front of the Information desk and refused to accept the situation, threatening to sue once morning broke, when the officials responsible came back on deck.

Responsible for the blizzard? You had to wonder. Up and down the main concourse, Lena paced, checked and rechecked the departure board, returned to the window, observed no change, and resumed pacing. Snow continued to fall. None of the fast food places seemed to be open at that hour—not that Lena was hungry but they would have given her something to do. The tourist shops were closed as well, so, except for the continuing whiteout at the big window, there was nothing to see, no distraction.

When she gave in and allowed herself to settle in one of the bucket chairs, she didn't expect to nap but imagined she might be able to relax. *Not a bit!* Unable to lean back or stretch her legs, she still hoped to close her eyes at least. But no such luck. When Lena first sat down, the woman sitting across from her had been drowsing, her infant deeply asleep in her lap. That quiet was not to last. The child woke abruptly and started screaming. Pacifier, bottle, burping were tried and refused—slapped away. Lena wasn't the only one to resent this. Angry glances were arrowed in the mom's direction—uselessly. What could anyone do? Empty chairs were scarce; the only alternative was the cold floor.

"She's teething," the mother apologized. Then announced proudly: "She's got three on top, two, and another one coming in, on the bottom. All ahead of schedule."

When the screaming did not abate and others left, Lena stood up and resumed pacing once again. And she kept on walking until, overcome with weariness, she imagined she'd be able to sleep anywhere. Then, in one of the bays she'd overlooked before, she lucked out—not one, but two chairs, were unoccupied and Lena seized them both, one for her carry-on, the other for her aching bones.

Having outlasted the book she'd brought along for the trip and hard up for something to occupy her mind, she opened a pamphlet she'd picked up in her wanderings. It seemed to be one of those motivational tracts. A pretty tale—about a silkworm suffering from some sort of blockage—the outlets through which gossamer was supposed to flow mysteriously plugged up. But the worm went on spinning filaments all the same, and when the invisible cocoon was finished, curled up, snugly wrapped in nothing at all, to sleep the sleep of transformation. And, in due course, the silkworm pupated and emerged as a butterfly. Right on schedule.

Sermon fodder, Lena said to herself—what Ed, her late husband, would have called "*pious piffle.*" She could hear him distinctly, summing up his thinking on the subject of faith: "Insufficient data for a meaningful answer." He'd said it often enough. Yet she's still surprised that she'd been so surprised by his goodness—not an unkind bone in his body—and without a speck of religion. Nothing like what she'd been brought up to expect. . . .

"Anything interesting?" asked the woman sitting one chair over.

"Not very," Lena said. "Just something somebody dropped." She'd be glad to pass it on, though.

"Oh, that's all right," the woman said and introduced herself as Rose. She was eager to strike up a conversation. "Helps kill time," she noted. She appeared to be about Lena's age and, as it turned out, she too was a recent widow. "How lucky is that!" she said, meaning (Lena assumed) that the two of them happened to meet. Rose did most of the talking.

So Lena learned how exhausting the past two years had been for Rose. Her husband's bitterness cut deep; he'd counted on being retired from the job he'd held—and hated—for as many years as he'd worked, living long enough to get back the time he'd put in. To get *even!* Unfortunately, that wasn't the way it happened: he'd worked for more than forty years and managed to survive a measly two after retirement. After he passed, Rose dragged herself around the apartment, stepping outside only when absolutely necessary. "Couldn't get my footing for months on end" was how she put it. Gathering up his things, going through his suit pockets before giving his clothes away to charity, she drifted, lost. Little things turning up, memories attached, like threads trailing, just about drove her crazy. Then, out of the blue, she'd won this travel lottery. Now she was off to see the country all expenses paid, trying to look on the bright side. Winning the lottery didn't compensate—nothing could—but at least it gave her something else to think about and got her out of the house. Her son was no help, tied up as he was with his wife's family.

Lena recognized the loneliness. How well she knew! And about becoming set in her widow-ways. Retired, alone in the house, she'd catch herself talking to Ed: "*How could you?*" Relying on one sleep-aid or another, she'd reason "It steadies me," knowing that Ed would not approve. She didn't know with how loud a voice she spoke her thoughts to him, having no answering voice to measure up against.

She and Ed both had decided against having children, their own or adopted, for reasons which seemed sensible at the time. They'd married late, for one. Both had teaching careers, hard-won professions, requiring post-graduate degrees, which meant years of day jobs and night school to qualify. Both were workaholics; there'd never been enough time.

Lena wouldn't allow herself to dwell on regret, and yet—*so much life unspent!* And, from time to time, she'd catch herself pondering the choices she'd made—or deferred, now forever foreclosed. Although she'd been a lifelong "book person," Lena found herself escaping to television, sometimes for hours at a stretch. She seemed to need the daily crises, the "concerning" or "disturbing" developments, even the disasters—the worse the better. She waited to hear Wolf Blitzer intone: "Our hearts go out. Our thoughts and prayers. . . ."

Our hearts go out. . . .

Unaccustomed to opening up to strangers, Lena hesitated before introducing herself to Rose. She gave her real name (well, actually, first and *middle* name) but improvised some of the other details. Theo became her brother. That wasn't much of a stretch—she'd always thought of him as her brother. He was ill and she was on her way west to tend to him. True enough. . . . But she did not say, "dying." She did not say "priest."

She made it clear that she didn't want to go into why Theo had never married, leaving Rose free to form her own conclusions. As they stared at the window, waiting for the curtain of snow to lift, they did their best to keep the conversation going. Sometimes it seemed a mere droning, like a dial tone. Then one or the other, Rose or Lena, nodding off momentarily, would draw herself up sharply with: "Sorry. Where were we?. . .You were saying?"

Flights resumed at the crack of dawn. After agreeing that they had a lot in common, that it was good they'd met, Lena and Rose somehow forgot to exchange full names and addresses before wishing each other well and turning to go their separate ways.

* * *

STANDING IN THE BEDROOM doorway, in silence, Lena studies Theo as he studies her. He does not appear to be ill. It's the house that seems to have suffered an attack, not simply stripped, but *plundered*.

Not a clock, not an image, not even a crucifix to anchor the drifting gaze. . . . The bookshelves are empty—*why?* He always loved books—it wasn't simply a question of decoration.

And how about the quilt that covers him? Someone must have brought this in from outside after he'd given away his own. It's faded pastel and Disney-themed, dotted with smiling chipmunks, lion cubs at play, dancing bears—hardly appropriate for an elderly priest. Meant for a child, it barely reaches his feet.

Why, she wants to cry out, *have you been shedding pieces of your life?*

Arm rigid, palm flat out: his first greeting. No welcome, but a clear enough warning: *Stop! Say it to the hand.* Not nice, but she's willing to wait for an opening. She's not in the mood to chatter anyway, she'd had enough of that with Rose.

When Lena ventures closer and stands at his bedside (Theo still saying not a word), it's a different story: reaching for her hand, his fingers close on hers and hold on with an iron grasp. Affection, surely. (He'd *asked* for her to come, after all.) *Still*—"unrelenting" is the word that comes to mind. This doesn't feel like the grip of a dying man. But the message is clear: *I have decided—there will be no appeal. You must support me.*

When she tries to free her hand, he pulls back, draws it to his chest. She can feel the pounding of his heart, how fast it is.

She'd been called by the chancery once they learned that Theo had stopped showing up for meals at the convent. Hadn't been seen by others for days. There were reports that he'd been leaving his garage door open day and night; anyone could enter at any time. Another concern was his last Mass, when he'd gone off-program. (Not their phrasing, but that was the gist.) He'd given a general anointing when he should have been preaching. Too many of the lay faithful seemed to assume that the act of anointing carried with it automatic absolution, although the absolution granted in such circumstances could have been only conditional at best. The canon lawyer for the diocese had sent a special emergency bulletin round to the parish to explain the difference.

About what he'd been reported to have said on that occasion, the diocese was reluctant to elaborate. Only this: He'd been mumbling as if talking to himself, as if he'd forgotten where he was. One of the complainants, who chose to remain anonymous, thought what he heard was: "God has grown dark to me." But he was sitting too far back to swear to it.

* * *

EVER SINCE SHE COULD remember Lena and Theo had been close, closer than first cousins if for no other reason than the fact that their mothers were twins. Lena had always thought of Theo as a brother. An older brother, since there were four years between them. She'd never been at all close to Simon, her real brother.

Of course there was no way for the diocese to know this. . . . Yet, mulling it over, Lena could come up with more than one reason the chancery might have turned to her. Coldly considered, there was the question of liability: she was there either to prevent self-harm by Theo—or, failing that, to witness that the diocese had done no harm to him. There were other practical reasons: *Best to keep such cases in the family*— publicity damage control, that sort of thing. Since Lena lived in Chicago and didn't know the locals here, she'd be less likely to gossip. Even the fact that she'd married outside the Church might have been a plus under the circumstances; perhaps they wanted someone who wouldn't be shocked.

But anyone thinking she might be able to change Theo's mind once he's set on something—*better think again*. . . . It's been two years since her last visit and she's struck by a sense of something in him—not so much changed as clarified. Whittled down to the core maybe. He does seem to have lost weight, but that's not it. . . .

Before, Lena liked to say she'd known him forever. He'd seemed little different from other kids—until he started spending too much time alone, keeping where he went and what he was thinking, to himself, hidden even from Lena. Something was clearly troubling him.

The one time he let her in on it, his question: "Is there a meaning to us?"—the way he put it—was foreign to her ears. They'd both been thoroughly catechized. The answer was ironclad, obvious: *God created us to love Him, to serve Him in this world, and to be happy with Him forever in the next.* How could there be more meaning than this?

Theo was all of fourteen—Lena, ten—when he announced that he wanted to go off to seminary and become a priest. Because she'd not seen it coming and because she knew how terribly she would miss him, she remained unconvinced by what he called his "reasons" for leaving. If he felt himself "called" by God, he never said a word about it. Instead, he gave a slew of excuses she couldn't bear to hear out. She suspected the main reason was his wanting to get off the farm, her own motive for leaving when the time came. Cotton was an unforgiving crop; chopping weeds and harvesting, stooped, or on your knees, dragging those long sacks behind you as they grew too heavy to lift, was back-breaking labor. Bracts and branches tore at your fingers as you tore out the bolls. There were no machines back then—and, anyway, who could afford them? Other crops—wheat, corn, milo—were friendlier, but required more water and, again, who could afford it?

There was another reason for his leaving that Lena shared—wanting an education. They lived in a pocket of the old country, their community named for the village their parents and grandparents left behind in Germany. Despite the openness of the country, the wide fields and unbounded Texas skies, Lena felt ever more constricted after Theo left. There was no one else she could talk to in a place where all questions, asked and unasked, had been answered for all time. To be sure, there was safety in it: the compass points were set; you could never, unless willfully, become lost. The known world was bounded by the iron fence of the parish cemetery containing nearly all their dead. Beyond it—disorder, the dragons of unbelief.

Growing up, Lena had never had a Protestant friend, never met a Jew. When she moved to the city, people found this hard to believe—Texas was, after all, part of the U.S.A, and wasn't the U.S.A. the melting pot of the world?

She couldn't credit his reasons back then, but she knew that Theo was determined to leave and that it was useless trying to stop him. What's more, he made her an accomplice, calling it "our secret," and for months she had to keep it that way. But she had not believed (or, again, was it—could not *bear* to believe?) that he'd go through with it. Then, on the morning he left, she'd slammed the car door on her own hand, smashing two fingers. She can still see—*feel*—where the injury was to this day. The family had been rushing, of course, to make sure Theo caught the bus on time, but she suspected it was no accident. She wept when he stepped up onto the bus, and the pain in her hand did not divert her.

They'd been so close, yet how had she missed what set him apart and on his separate path? She kept coming back to this. It wasn't his name. There'd been a number of "Theo's" in the family, none of them priests, none especially devout. What, then, singled him out from the other children? Only one difference Lena could recall: a need to be quiet. Abruptly, in the middle of their games, he'd take off. *Nothing so unusual in that, was there?*

He'd certainly not worn out his knees with praying beforehand; mortification of the flesh was never a motive. In recent years, he liked to say that the Church hierarchy was his only hair shirt. He put up with the frustrations that came with the territory—he didn't seek out suffering.

Nor had he seemed especially attentive at Mass. As an altar server, he'd been accused of "daydreaming" and scolded repeatedly for his timing in ringing the Sanctus bells. But. . .come to think of it, maybe that *was* a sign. Far from dreaming, he was never too slow in sounding the bells but overeager rather, too quick to anticipate.

Years ago, she'd asked Theo, "Didn't you ever want to marry?" He'd answered without hesitation, "Of course. It wouldn't have meant anything if I'd given up nothing I valued." Useless to press or ask again. They'd been schooled on how to answer—how *not* to answer. She never asked outright "Have you found what you were looking for?" For however mixed his reasons for becoming a priest might have been, the years after leaving home changed him. Something changed him—he'd found *something*. And repetition reinforced it. "Holy monotony" (as he dubbed it) became habit. And slowly but surely, as a way of walking shapes a shoe, habit shaped character, and character—a life.

Her own life followed a different course. As a single woman. she'd had to wait until she reached eighteen before she could leave without scandal, then wandered for years, finding her way by trial and error. It gave Lena pause sometimes to think that she has traveled so far from home—farther even than Theo—who, after all, has spent his life in rural and small town parishes and never left the Church.

But, back then, when Theo left she was sure of so little. They'd been children together. When he stepped up onto that bus, she feared she'd never see him again. In a sense, she never did.

And yet here she was—he'd written her down as "next of kin." She'd been called.

* * *

SHE'D BEEN WARNED beforehand that Theo had given away nearly everything he owned, and that he'd excused his few remaining possessions as being "on loan." These included two folding chairs, a typing chair on wheels, and the armchair-recliner in the living room—all together, barely able to seat the small delegation of priests who gather to greet Lena on the afternoon of her arrival.

The fathers are in various states of clerical undress: one in sports jacket, plaid shirt, brown corduroy pants, and black oxfords; another, in white shirt, black below the waist; the two others: all black, but with collars unfastened. "I'm Father Kamin—Al Kamin," says the one in civvies, extending a warm hand.

If there were one more person, someone would have had to stand back up against the wall, or perch on Theo's desk. The desk, gunmetal-grey, salvaged from one of the chancery offices, is the unlovely centerpiece of the room. Two of the priests, coming inside—for the first time in a while, apparently—stop and stare. In their faces, the same bewilderment appears, the same question: *Why?*

There are theories. Father Kamin reasons that it's "that old German surfacing again. Control!—Discipline! No unfinished business!" He recalls that when Father Theo was Chancellor of the diocese he never left the office until he had everything squared away, not a scrap of paper left on top of his desk.

Another father (whose name Lena doesn't catch) invokes the usual piety: "We take nothing with us, after all." But then, out of the blue: "I believe his heart's torn, someway."

Theo *seemed* to be sleeping when the fathers arrived but Lena wasn't sure of this. The house is so cramped, his living room and bedroom so close together, he must have been within earshot. Nothing that was said would have hurt him to overhear, though.

"It happened so gradually," Father Nolan puts in. "He never was what you'd call 'gregarious' and less so after he retired." Little patience for small talk—fewer and fewer visitors. No big dramatic changes. "It took months before we started to worry about it. I blame myself. Should've checked in on him more often."

"One thing," he muses, "all the while he was stripping the house down, he kept adding to his garden," ordering new bulbs, laying chips of pine bark over last season's hay mulch, putting down nametags—and what names! You'd find him on his knees, outdoors whenever he could be, praying and fussing over that little parcel of ground."

"Ever a farmer," Father Kamin says.

"Ever a prayerful man, a saintly man," Father Ryan says.

To which Lena can't help adding: "Ever a stubborn man."

"Saintly *and* stubborn," Father Ryan corrects her. "Sure, and don't the two go together? Saint Francis, now. Pick any saint you please . . ." And he dithers on about Saint Lawrence selling the sacred vessels from his church to give to the poor.

Lena doesn't know about "saintly" but could tell you plenty about stubborn! A streak of sheer mulishness runs in the family. She's reminded of Theo's father refusing hearing aids when the family gave him the money as a birthday gift and begged him to at least give them a try. "I've heard enough!" he declared—and heard little more for the rest of his life.

Another thing: The good fathers seem to be unaware of the fact that Theo's breviary is missing—mislaid or given away. Lena noticed this right away, because where could it be? The bookshelves are empty, his bed table is bare. But she's not about to bring this to anyone's attention. His breviary has been a constant companion since seminary days. More than once (with a twinkle in his eye) he'd called it "the wife." With his breviary goes the saying of his daily office—what was one to make of *that*? Then again, Lena corrects herself, by now he hardly needs written prompts—not for those prayers closest to his heart.

Sister Perpetua stops by minutes after the fathers leave. She refuses to sit down—she won't be staying—only wants to greet Lena and ask whether there's anything she needs. And to vent a little about a dream troubling the older sisters, a "premonition." Something about black and white cattle. . .a dangerous crossing. . .Theo leading. . . Lena fails to make sense of the garbled dream, she is far too tired to try.

Soon after this, Dr. Foster looks in.

"I don't usually make house calls," he explains. "I'm here now more as a personal friend. . . . Though—I must say—having a friendly conversation has been getting harder and harder lately. Mostly, he seems to be talking *around* me—if he talks at all. . . . I don't understand what's brought him to this point. He appears healthy enough for his age. He could have years coming to him yet—I simply don't know. We'd have to take him into the hospital and run a battery of tests to be able to say what's really going on. But he's refused to go to the hospital this time and he has the right to. Still, I keep thinking: *Had we admitted him. . . .*"

They are standing just outside the bedroom right then and Theo must be awake, and clearly he's been listening. "Had we had rain. . . ." he says. "Had we had wheat. . . ."

"A mild dementia, might be," the doctor adds.

But Lena disagrees. She knows exactly what Theo means when he says, "Had we had rain."

"It's perfectly reasonable. Enough moisture, a different crop, and he might have stayed on the farm—everything might have gone differently for him," she argues. "I understand what he's saying. He's mulling over the past. He's depressed, that's all."

"Well, might be," the doctor says doubtfully. "But depression is also serious, with real physical effects. Anyway—his mind seems to be made up."

Dr. Foster surveys the room as he speaks. The empty shelves. The walls so stark. Only the pocked traces of nail holes, the mottle of faded and unfaded patches newly uncovered, to stare at and wonder about and, if you could, remember.

* * *

THEY'RE IN FOR THE evening when Father Kamin calls and insists on bringing over a small rental television. "Puzzling, isn't it. . .? He's still connected after giving his set away. Probably intended to cancel before the billing date at the end of the month. Could be he simply forgot. It would be good if you could persuade him to give it a glance. A distraction might help, might draw him out of himself—there's still a chance he might change his mind before it's too late. I've been urging him to get a pet for a long time now. A disrupter is what he needs—a puppy, just the thing. Everyone needs a love object. Or a hobby, at least. At one point he talked about woodworking, making birdhouses, something along those lines . . . I'm not convinced he's as sick as he seems to think he is."

"And besides," he adds, testing the remote as channel after channel flashes by, "at least *you* won't lose touch with the world. It's entirely possible in a place like this."

Father Kamin is already on his feet, preparing to leave, when he adds: "I don't know what rumors might be going round, but eventually you'll probably pick up some fuss or complaint. About his doing things differently—sins of style, you might say. Theo's been on the receiving end of plenty of petty backbiting, as who hasn't? Death by a hundred bites—or nibbles, really, not worth mentioning. Your brother has an uncomfortable habit of speaking his mind and, when he hits home, people don't forget it."

Which makes Lena wonder.

* * *

LENA IS LOCKING UP for the night when Theo calls out to her: "I never do that. I close it, but never lock it. Nothing here anybody'd want to steal."

"*I'm* here," Lena reminds him. "And I'm ready to call it a day. . . . Down like a stone and up like a loaf!" Then, recalling both their mothers saying this, they both laugh. A surprise to Lena—Theo can still laugh.

Right now what she wants most is to put her feet up, and the living room armchair—what Theo still calls (country fashion) his "kick-back chair"—will do perfectly. She's a little surprised, but grateful, that Theo allowed the chair to remain. Tomorrow, she'll have to borrow a blanket from the convent next door. For tonight, she'll throw on her coat as a cover.

She does sleep, but brokenly, in snatches, remaining watchful, despite the fact that Theo stirs not at all.

3

THEN AND NOW

TOWARDS MORNING LENA hears—*thinks* she hears—Theo murmur: "Let's turn back now."

"You're dreaming out loud," she answers, then wonders: *Could he be starting to have second thoughts? If so—*

One of the home health nurses who's been hired to look in on Theo urges Lena to keep a record. There's not much to report. For what it's worth—

> *Tuesday—Supper 7:30*
> *sip of chicken soup*
> *bite of pie*
>
> *Wednesday—*
> *6:30 a.m. awakes needs help*
> *7:30 spoonful oatmeal*
>
> *Lunch—*
> *chicken soup—refused*

"Do me a favor—one sip," Lena pleads. Then scolds: "You must eat!"

"Why?" he asks. "Why must I?" Moving by stealth, Lena seizes advantage of his speaking mouth to advance the spoon past his lips. *No go*—his jaws lock, she hits a barrier of clenched teeth, he gags on nothing. Again—*be quick!*—sneak follow-up—his hand strikes back—the spoon clatters to the floor. Beside herself, Lena cries out: "You *can't* do this!"—her voice breaking.

An accident—unintended, she tells herself. *It's not at all like him. Meaning only to brush the spoon away, his hand must have swerved; his movements are clumsy now, he has less and less control—*

"All right, I won't pressure you," she's actually shaking—she wants to shake him. She knows it was deliberate.

Time out. Take ten.

"Think about what you're doing. I'll give you time to reconsider—surprise me!" and, after plumping Theo's pillows—*could he be smiling?*—she withdraws to the kitchen to cool down.

Inhale. Exhale. She clocks herself. Ten minutes is all she can stand. But she returns to find nothing has changed. Sensing she's about to speak, Theo cuts her off the same way he did when she first entered his house: arm rigidly extended, palm perpendicular, flat out: *Stop! Say it to the hand.*

End of discussion, she thinks. *It's over before it begins!*

The soup remains untouched. *I could warm it up for you,* she thinks, but knows it would be useless. The fact that, once or twice, only yesterday, he opened his mouth when a spoon was pressed to his lips counts for nothing—simply the fact that old habits become automatic over time. Or the fact that sometimes it takes too much energy to resist.

Sister Perpetua has a new strategy. Calling it a "strategy" makes it sound calculated—it isn't. Lena has no doubt that she believes with her whole heart what she is about to say. Clearing a space for his supper tray on the already-cluttered nightstand and drawing a chair up close to the bed, she confides to Theo that she has prayed to the founder of her order, Mother Bernarda, and received a promise in reply: The cloud that lies so heavily on Father Theo's spirit will be lifted. He will return to the land of the living and start to eat once again. "Mother's voice—it was like a whisper," she explains, the soft, motherly voice of an elderly woman with a foreign accent, speaking the words slowly with wide spaces in-between. When the voice faded, Sister Perpetua felt a strong twisting in her gut.

Theo's eyes remain resolutely, willfully, shut, but he's listening and somehow managing to see—to Lena there's no question he's awake. He clenches his teeth when sister raises the spoon a final time. "It won't happen today," she concedes after a third attempt. "But I believe in miracles. I'll be back."

At least Theo is still drinking. *Or is he?* He no longer sips from a straw but sucks whatever moisture can be squeezed from a small sponge on a stick, a swab meant for mouth cleaning when toothpaste becomes too harsh. Sometimes he holds on with such powerful suction that Lena has a hard time freeing it from between his clenched teeth. To this extent he is still clinging to life.

Lena struggles to put her finger on how Theo's changed since the last time she visited. He was definitely heavier then, his color good, spirits high. He'd been spending a good deal of time outdoors in his semi-retirement, gardening and planting trees, enjoying his leisure. They'd gathered for the anniversary of his ordination, marking the midpoint between his Golden and Diamond Jubilees. He'd insisted on keeping the "fuss" to a minimum and had absolutely forbidden anyone in the family or parish to bring gifts. "I don't want this to be a shakedown of the faithful," as he put it. It turned out to be as he wished—a simple and joyful celebration, with the higher-ups busy elsewhere.

That was three years back, Ed also in apparent good health.

Lena knows she's in for sleepless night. The chair is not to blame—it's comfortable enough. And it's not as if she expects her help will be required that often right yet. Theo is still able to get himself up and to the bathroom unassisted. If he persists in the course he seems determined and becomes too weak to lift himself from the bed, she has only to ask for male assistance—parish volunteer or professional. She cannot lift him on her own.

So Lena sits in the semi-dark, surfing the channels, picking up the news of the day in scraps. Low volume (listening for Theo), depending on closed

captioning subtitles for making sense of what she's seeing. Images—phantoms—flash, flicker, fade. Now the
captions say they're talking, now singing actual words,
now simply "scatting."

Mostly it's escape she's seeking. It reminds her
of the time—it went on for weeks, actually—after Ed
died. Full volume—so the voice followed her from
room to room. It was company, and when she settled
in front of it, it became a hearth fire, emitting warmth
and light.

Now, moving from channel to channel, she lands
on a story about a little girl caught up in a war zone
somewhere in the Middle East (it goes by too fast
to catch exactly where). The child has learned to clap
when the bombs fall around her; she has learned to
clap but can no longer speak. Just then . . . Lena thinks
she hears Theo stirring—

She shifts abruptly to another channel, a nature
program. An elephant is leading her clan to water. It's
a "she," Lena is surprised to learn, a matriarch—an an-
cient lady, scored with wrinkles. Wrinkles on the wrinkles. To show the members of the flock the direction
they must turn, she brushes the ground lightly with
one foot, a motion so subtle humans might miss it.

After long journeying over parched land, she has
led them to water, this lady Moses, and now it is time
for her to go off—alone—to die. Her followers enter
the water and spray themselves, they trumpet water,
their gray flesh darkens. Will they mourn their leader?
But they seem not to notice that she has left them.

"Turn it up!"—comes from the bedroom. But when she rouses herself to go check on Theo, he appears to be sound asleep. *Must've imagined it—*

So it's back to humans and breaking news. It's too much happening too fast: a tenement in New York burning, a woman weeping for someone trapped inside, an ad for Kentucky Fried Chicken, a rally in Bangladesh. The advertisements roll on. Now: It's total commitment to Diet Shake. Now: A man pursued by waltzing bears is touting a laxative called "Morning Ease." Now: A man and a woman are throwing pies at each other. Whipped cream covers their faces, splatters their chests. An invisible audience laughs, so this is funny, apparently. Now without transition or pause, the same man and the woman are shooting at one another. Where do the guns come from? No one expected this. The invisible audience gives an audible gasp. Now the paramedics have arrived, the bodies are being bundled, their faces covered. . . .

Does this actually happen, or is it only reality t.v., or does she dream it? The television runs on, phantasmagoria streaming. She's adrift in the borderland between sleep and waking—how to tell one from the other?—it's all delirium.

When Lena opens her eyes next it's to a blank screen and a laugh track going. She'd neglected to put the kick-back chair as far back as it could go and wakes feeling like a rusty hinge. Adjusting the chair to full reclining position and stretching out, she welcomes the dark.

4

"STUFF!"

MORNING.

Up and out! Up and doing! Lena urges herself on. But there is nowhere to go and nothing doing—or, at least, nothing useful to be done right now. While Theo sleeps, Lena paces.

She misses particularly the shadow box lined with black velvet that used to hang over the fireplace. In it, a crudely hammered spoon and fork, bent from decades of use, gave testimony to the hard times their grandparents endured, to their survival against the odds. Those, Lena was to learn, had gone to John David, a great nephew still living and farming at the old homestead, an arrangement which made sense, the only one, it seemed to her, that did.

But—how to account for the rest?

Lena takes it personally. She can't help feeling it. The poverty of the place is a rebuke to memory, to creature comfort, a rebuke to family and professional pride.

A rebuke to beauty. The very walls seem stricken—only pale patches and nail holes remaining to mark the missing. Even the light switch covers have disappeared. Lena had never really noticed them before and is only now alerted to the fact that they'd existed by the ghost traces they've left behind. They must have been ornamented in some way.

Missing: the carvings and wall crosses, the Rublev icon (a rare, particularly fine, reproduction, which happened to be a gift from her). The olive wood cross with its self-replicating arms had been one of Ed's favorites. Her husband, though an unbeliever, had tried to explain to Theo his own fascination with the Jerusalem cross the last time they'd visited—something about fractal diagrams and recursive functions. Lena knew how utterly foreign and lacking in context such comments would be for Theo, but he'd listened politely and made no remark.

And Lena misses the brightly colored Byzantine cross with its languid floating Christ. It was unusually cheerful—too cheerful maybe for Theo in his latest mood.

Also banished: the candlesticks and bookends, the framed certificates in Latin and English, the awards. All his books. . . *("I'll drown my book. . .").* Lena's thoughts keep circling back to this—*how could he?* He always loved to read.

He's given away his stationary exercise bicycle (his "going-nowhere bike") prescribed to keep his heart rate regular.

In recent years, "stuff!" had grown to be a favorite expression with him; Lena wasn't the only one who'd noticed. She'd heard his rant on ecclesial finery before, it wasn't a new theme. "White rochets and red cassocks, zuchettos, birettas, capes, miters, rings and white gloves." Cincture, amice, maniple—all doomed for the dustbin of history, the sooner the better. These views of his must have been well known: he'd never become a bishop, let alone a monsignor.

So, all right, she reasons, *he's done with ornamentation, luxuries, extras. He'll keep essentials only. . . .* But— *again*—that fails to explain why he'd want to banish books.

There remain two black suits, one shiny, greenish with wear, two pairs of black shoes with ground-down heels, one bed with bed table, eyeglasses and reading glasses, one table lamp, one standing lamp, desk, office chair, and recliner. Two dishtowels. A few mismatched plates and cups, teakettle. A jumble of cutlery. Lena realizes that in much of the world this would count as God's plenty, but Texas is not a third world country.

There's a jar with coins and a few single bills on the kitchen counter—stash for handouts, she suspects.

She's heard that he'd tried to give back his car, a retirement gift from Holy Name, his last parish. Luckily, the parish council voted to return the car to him "for the time being." This is convenient for Lena since, having flown down from Chicago, she's carless. She'll need a car to get around—to get *out.*

5

PROVOCATIONS

SHE *HAS* TO GET OUT. Lena needs reassurance that the world as she's known it continues to exist. Television keeps her up on the big news—everything going to hell in a hand-basket—not that anything ever truly changes. Theo hasn't yet canceled his subscription to the daily paper but Lena expects he'll get around to it once he remembers. That's. . .*if* he remembers. Lena is not about to bring it up, although it matters little to her whether the paper keeps coming or not. Since she's never lived here, most of the local news is lost on her.

Groceries give her a good excuse to go. One of the sisters from the convent is visiting and happy to sit bedside until she returns.

Lena hasn't entirely given up with trying to coax Theo back to eating. There still might be a chance. The latest is this crazy idea, more of a mantra than idea, really—*maybe salmon patties, he used to love salmon patties. . . .* But she loses conviction after listing the ingredients. She'd need breadcrumbs, eggs, oil, chives and dill—to reconstitute the kitchen is what it amounts to. She decides to ask the sisters to give it a try, instead.

And they do. By suppertime, the cook from the convent brings over a platter: salmon patties, green beans, and mashed potatoes. All to be inherited by Lena—Theo refuses to touch a thing.

Early next morning, Dr. Foster drops by to check Theo's vital signs. When Lena walks him to the door he indicates that he wants to say something to her out of Theo's hearing. So they step out into the garden. He glances around and reads off a couple of labels and, smiles: "Never heard of such. Did he make them up? Was he serious?" Lena shrugs—she has no idea and, clearly, is in no mood to be distracted. "What can anyone do?" she asks. "What can *I* do?"

"You know him. Once he's made up his mind—" Dr. Foster shrugs. "Just be there."

"You've got to realize," he goes on, "that anyone can go at any time. All you have to do is to just stop eating. Believe me, there are worse ways to go. It's faster if you stop drinking as well, but likely to be more painful. It's not all that uncommon for some elderly or terminally ill people to simply quit. I haven't had that much experience with priests but I don't have to remind you that priests are people, aging men with the usual prostate and other problems, nobody exempt. I've been in practice for over thirty years, seen medicine take great strides in my time. But there are limits. We've learned how to patch on extra months, years sometimes, not necessarily good ones—"

Lena interrupts: "What do people die of when they 'simply quit,' as you put it?"

"Renal failure, often." Of Theo in particular he says: "It. . .the process. . .may take some time. Your brother has a strong heart." Then he adds: "Once hospice checks in, I'll be checking out."

* * *

SUNDAY: INSTEAD OF celebrating Mass, or getting up to meet the morning, Theo rises briefly to splash some water on his face, then goes straight back to bed. He has not shaved in days, and will not let anyone do it for him.

One of the deacons—Elias—stops by to bring Communion. He breaks off only a small fragment, smaller than his thumbnail, from the Host. If Theo persists in not eating as he seems determined to do, soon he'll be unable to swallow even a fraction of that fragment. Beyond the fact that he hasn't visited for some time, Elias makes no comment on the bareness of the walls and shelves, but Lena catches him staring and knows he is aching to ask.

Abruptly, he turns to Lena, pyx in hand. "How about you?"

She makes the gesture of respectful refusal, arms crossed, palms to her shoulders; then to soften her refusal she dips her head for his blessing.

In the daytime, Theo lies on top of his fully made bed (not *in* it—Lena has succeeded in making a point of this). She's smoothed the sheets and tucked the quilt in tight. And she keeps the door between bedroom and living room open so she can keep checking that he isn't creeping back under the covers. After the deacon leaves, she tries reading to him. The local paper is full of church news and Sunday feature stories—surely, she thinks, one of them will engage him.

How about this? A competition for raising the tallest yard cross. Baptist (anodized aluminum) versus Assembly of God (wood). The Baptist, an engineer by trade, has been leading with a twenty-two foot structure. Now a third party from one of the big non-denominational Christian fellowships is reported to be raising funds for an even taller cross, material unspecified. Passions are running high and the police are on standby alert.

Does Theo care? Is he even listening? He raises no objection, voices no question, doesn't even bother to laugh. He's awake, eyes wide open, but his face remains impassive.

Surely one of these. . . . Still hoping to get a rise out of him, Lena reads out from the choicest *Letters to the Editor*. She figures Theo is bound to recognize at least one of the names of the people writing in.

"Did you know that Jesus was a Republican?"

Is that a faint hoot or "hmpf" she hears in reply?

She keeps on: "In case you're wondering. . . . It's backed up by Proverbs, chapter 20, verse 2: *'There is treasure to be desired and oil in the dwelling of the wise, but a foolish man spendeth it up.'"*

The letter is lengthy, so Lena paraphrases: "Because the government is busy taking from the wise and redistributing to the foolish, more than half the population fails to take it upon themselves to care for the poor and widows. It's all the fault of big government pretending to be Jesus."

That gets a rise out of Lena at least. Another letter, equally preposterous, follows; she can't help editorializing, interjecting "incredible!" then reading aloud the editor's submission instructions: "'All letters are edited for length, logic, libel, and taste.'"

"Can you imagine what the *rejects* look like?" she says, laughing.

But Theo isn't joining in. He seems to be studying his hands.

"What makes you think you're dying right now?" Lena asks.

"I *know* I am."

"You mean you've *decided?*"

"Think what you like."

To help matters not at all, later in the afternoon, a young woman comes to the door bringing a letter. "It's urgent," she explains. The letter is loosely folded, without an envelope, privacy apparently not a concern. No, she doesn't want to come in: "I hear he's taken to his bed," she says, her lower lip trembling. "At his last Mass—when—" she can't go on. All she wants is for Lena to pass her letter on to Father so he'll be sure to deliver it to her Momma and Poppa when he gets to heaven.

It burns Lena's fingers. Handing the letter to Theo, she notes only that the scrawl is loopy and childish, the lines slanting steeply uphill. Theo glances at it, then reaches for his glasses to read it again, then passes it back over to her—"You should read this," his only comment. "You sure?" she asks. "I want you to," he insists. Lena doesn't know whether he hopes to convince her that faith like this still exists, or to prove (yet again) that he is dying, everyone knows it.

Once again, he examines his hands. Turning them over, he studies the blue splotches that look like bruises, covering their backs. "Grave mold," he pronounces.

"Nonsense. You were taking blood-thinners recently, weren't you? Before this? Blood-thinners are anti-coagulants—there's some minor bleeding under the skin."

Lena holds the letter by her fingertips. *Surely Theo isn't taken in by this, not even tempted.* More than once he'd confided to Lena how he pictured heaven: "It's not fairy dust, harps, luminous clouds, any of that. And I don't believe there's a *where* there. It's a state of being at the end—being in a right relationship with God and the people around you. The point being: Make it right—here, now, on earth." Lena can live with that. She hopes he's not retreating now.

Stalled in the doorway, letter still in hand, she's at a loss where to stash it, though. Theo gestures in the general direction of his desk. She doesn't want to leave the thing floating around topside, so decides to tuck it away in one of the drawers.

She's astonished to find the drawer half-full. Has Theo overlooked this? Or did he intend to clear it out at a later date, once he found the energy? Lena makes a mental note to look into it; she'll wait for a time when Theo is sleeping, bringing whatever she finds to his attention after she has a chance to look it over on her own first.

6

FOUND ITEMS

HE'S TAKEN NO NAP earlier so Lena assumes that his first sleep will be sound and unbroken. But she keeps her ear tuned for the faintest stirring.

Here's her chance to check out the desk drawers. Yes, she is poking around in his personal business—*snooping*, some might say. Yes, but it's in a good cause. He's not talking, so how can she hope to reach him unless she knows more? She moves stealthily, though.

Copies of complaints sent to the chancery—there's a bunch. . . .

He's been too harsh, preaching on "our larcenous hearts—mine and yours." The complainant remembered the phrasing but could no longer recall the context, the occasion prompting it. *It must be admitted,* the letter went on, *that Father said this in passing and applied it first of all to himself.*

He's been too soft, "spinning the Gospel", renaming the parable of the prodigal son as "the parable of the prodigal father" in one instance. There are comments in Theo's hand scrawled below: *No "spin". And not in the least original with me. What is this parable about if not the father, our Father, lavish in love, prodigal in forgiveness?*

This—on the back of an official diocesan form, complainant unnamed—citing chapter and verse (2 Timothy, 4:2): *Preach the word, be urgent, in season, out of season. Convince, rebuke, exhort.*

There's more—

Reports of "liturgical irregularities", most particularly, the substitution of a general anointing for the homily he did not deliver at his most recent Mass. Reference is made to an earlier complaint sent to the chancery.

How long, Lena asks herself, *has he been under surveillance?*

And then she recalls the last time she'd been summoned here to tend to him. Ed was still alive, but already seriously ill, so she hadn't been able to come. Later, she learned that Theo had been delirious, running a 104 degree fever, although no one had known that before the police stepped in. Hard to believe that was little over a year ago—he seemed to recover so quickly and sounded so well over the phone.

It had been a hard winter, the coldest night of a cold December, snow underfoot and snow falling. He'd been alone, inside the house. Needing help with the furnace, but not wanting to disturb the sisters asleep in the convent, he'd set off, trekking across a field to seek help from the houses with Christmas lights in the distance. Without jacket, hat, or gloves. Bedroom slippers. Knocking on door after door, no one took him in. "But how could anyone blame them?" he'd explained to Lena.

Out of his priestly uniform—a stranger lost, stumbling through the snow—no one recognized him. His burning face, dishevelment, and incoherence marked him as a drunk. Finally, someone called the police.

The explanation for this incident—infection, high fever, purely physical causes—seemed reasonable enough and was not pursued further.

But back to his desk—

Item: Note to himself on his years in ministry: *Remember all the graciousness you've received—be what you have received.*

Item: Letter to the Chancery, directed to the Vicar General, outlining the instructions for his funeral, signed and dated by Theo only a month ago:

I ask that Father Garner be in charge of liturgical arrangements. I wish to be vested in a simple alb.

I ask that the pallbearers be. . . . The names are unfamiliar to Lena.

Item: Handful of old photos, some labeled, some not. A spotted dog from their childhood they called "Buckle" because he liked to chew leather belts. A photo of Theo as an infant in his mother's arms, his face half-swallowed by the shadow of the poke bonnet he's wearing. Boys and girls alike wore poke bonnets at a certain age. Theo, if it is Theo, seems to be gazing in fascination at his bare toes. On the other hand, it could have been herself, Lena reflects, their mothers, after all, were twins—not identical, but enough alike to be often mistaken for one another.

Their mothers were alike in so many other ways, Lena recalls. Their fierce piety, above all. Like still insisting on meatless Fridays after the rules of the Church changed and other people were moving on. For their family, it was fish on Friday from the foundation of the world, fish on Friday forever.

But—what's this? Rain gauge readings to the hundredth of an inch. Annual totals. His comment: *Last spring driest on record. TIME & TEMPERATURE:* the phone number for the local weather station spelled out with minor variations, horizontally and vertically, over and over.

392–2261	3
	9
392–2611	2
	6
	1
3–9–2–2–9–1–1	1

It was the old farmer surfacing in him, Lena guesses. Or was he testing his memory—afraid he was losing it?

More jottings:

> *Papa said "I've heard enough!" when he refused hearing aids and chose to remain deaf for the last years of his life. (Everyone was willing—eager—to*

chip in and pay for it.) There's a stubborn streak,
runs in the family, we all have it.
        For my part, I've spoken enough.

On a 2x2 Post-It note:

The Word became flesh, became words
Paved over with words

Then Lena thinks she hears him call her name. She isn't sure. He might be simply shifting position in bed. But enough for now. Gently, she slides the drawer shut.

7

VISITORS

FRANK HESITATES IN THE doorway, stamping his dusty farmer's boots.

"C'mon in! Don't bother," Lena waves him inside. "The doormat's gone. As you can see. Same with the rugs that used to be inside—he gave them away, I'm told."

Cousin Frank, Theo's youngest brother, arrives without notice. He claims to be scouting a certain seed company nearby and, while he happens to be in the area, it occurs to him: why not drop in? A spur of the moment impulse as he would have it. Lena knows better. You don't drive ten hours, five each way—for *seeds*—when there are plenty of enterprising seed companies out where he lives. Clearly, he's fishing for firsthand news, something to report back to the rest of the family. Whatever he's heard must have alerted him to trouble.

Taking his first look around inside, he gives a low whistle of surprise: "What in the world? Looks like he's moved out. What's going on?" Lena confesses she doesn't know. No one here does. She's not willing to repeat Dr. Foster's mention of "a mild dementia" even as a possibility. In the absence of hospital tests, he assured her, any stab at diagnosis was bound to be speculative. Lena suspects that most medical labels would miss the particular knot Theo is struggling to untangle, in any case. Yet she feels certain at least of this much: Theo may have "moved out" but he's living in; he isn't fading, but intensifying; not wandering, but concentrating.

"Since *when* has this been going on?" Frank wants to know. "We've been talking by phone pretty much once a week. Just last week his voice sounded strong as ever, just a little . . . maybe . . . anxious." He stands just inside the door, lacing and unlacing his fingers, hoping for enlightenment that Lena's unable to provide. He's brought along his grandson (Lena's grand-nephew) Daniel, and Max, Daniel's new pet, a mongrel with some long-haired breed in the mix. Lena ushers the three of them into the bedroom where Theo, propped up by pillows, half-sits, half-reclines on the bed.

Frank tries his best to rustle up conversation, with no more success than anyone else who's tried. "We do like you tell us to," he says finally. It's spoken with a wink, but Lena knows it for a fact—*they do*.

Meantime, Daniel and Max have hopped up on the bed. Max snuggles between Daniel and Theo, angling for a full, wet, kiss on Theo's lips. Theo sketches a wobbly sign of the cross over them, blessing them both. Max licks his fingers in reply.

Daniel must be seven—or eight. Or is it nine? Ten, even? It's hard to tell with him, and Lena has not kept up. He's still in his milk teeth, no signs of permanent teeth coming in. Since birth he's been seriously undersized ("off the charts for an American child"), then slow at learning—"developmentally challenged" in the peculiar jargon of the schools. He's brought a gift for this visit: a handmade crucifix of bare unpolished wood, the tiny figure of twisted metal, a sagging Y-shape at its center, unmistakable. One arm, Lena noticed, is loose, must've been pulled. "He has to stay on those sticks!" Daniel warns. Then, as if Theo is about to challenge this, he bursts into tears: "No! He *has* to stay—he has to!"

"What do we call those sticks, Danny?" Frank prompts. "Remember? Cr—?"

"Sticks!" Daniel repeats. "Oh, I know—crossticks!"

Lena invites them to sit down in the kitchen, offering Frank a cup of coffee, and milk and cookies for Daniel, before they hit the road again. It's a bold, completely rash, offer. Theo's is a far from normal household, less so now than ever before. Lena knows there's a carton of milk in the fridge, a kettle on the stove, cup on the sideboard, but beyond that—cookies?

Fortunately, the jar of instant coffee is not entirely depleted, and a frantic search of the cupboard reveals a box with a few remaining oatmeal cookies, likely to be stale, but she'll urge Daniel to dunk them, which he does. Frank sips coffee and fills Lena in on the latest family news. Max paws their knees under the table, begging for crumbs.

Then, abruptly, Frank leaves them. Lena overhears indistinct murmurs from the bedroom (only one voice), most likely an attempt by Frank to persuade Theo to come to the table. The outcome is foredoomed and Frank returns to the kitchen all too quickly.

"Seems to be wanting to sleep," he reports.

Frank's aged, Lena thinks. *But no doubt he's thinking the same of me.*

With Frank clearly discouraged, Daniel becomes increasingly lively. He kicks the table leg , kicks again and misses. Max gives a yelp, the table shudders—Frank glowers. "I didn't do it," Daniel insists. "My shoe did."

"How many times do I have to tell you? " Frank says. "Your foot is in your shoe. Your foot moves your shoe. Your head moves your foot."

"My head?"

"Yes, your head, like I told you before. We have to be quiet in here."

Suddenly Daniel drops to the floor and disappears. He crouches under the table, hugging Max. Frank's voice is threatening: "Get up! You are not a dog—quit acting like one!"

"I have to tell Max I'm sorry," Daniel mumbles.

"Up, up! No more excuses—do as you're told!" Frank warns.

Resurfacing, Daniel turns to Lena. "Do you like being you?"

"Danny!" Frank objects. "What kind of question is that?"

"But *do* you?"

"Most times," Lena says. But then he's on to something else: "Can I have more cookie?"

Frank agrees to his having one—only one—more: "What do we say?"

"Please! Please! Please!" begs Daniel. "That will make your third cookie," Frank reminds him.

"At school we clap three times and put our heads down on the desk," says Daniel.

Lena cannot think—nor can Frank, apparently— of where to go with this.

"Am I getting big?"

"That's right," Frank answers. "You're getting bigger."

"Almost bigger," says Daniel.

"Remember what I told you—why we're given two ears but only one mouth? We have to be quiet in here. This is like a church."

Daniel shakes his head: "Don't look like church," but Frank, having other more pressing things on his mind, leaves off and turns to Lena. "What's *really* going on with Theo?" he slaps the table for emphasis. "That's what I want to know." When Lena shrugs he says something that surprises her: "I'm glad you're here. If he'll talk to anybody, it's you."

"He's not really talking."

"But maybe he will. What bothers me most is: How could he come this far and—?"

Lena doesn't have to spell out the rest of his question—she's been asking herself the same thing.

"How am I to explain this to the rest of the family?"

This is an altogether different question, of course. Lena has no idea.

After they leave, Theo turns to Danny's crucifix, lifting it and bringing it close to his eyes. (*Don't say a word*—Lena reminds herself.) And there, on the bed table next to his folded glasses, which he taps from time to time but no longer wears, he sets it down and it remains.

This he's allowed to remain.

More visitors. The bishop knocks and presents himself bedside. Lena wonders what *he* makes of the bare walls and shelves, and the borrowed Disney quilt, disreputable in itself, now sprinkled with dog hairs. It shouldn't be hard to read the bishop's thoughts. He makes a small mouth, withholding speech. Then, tapping his ring, his pectoral cross, seeming to draw strength from these emblems, he clears his throat and proclaims: "Our help is in the name of the Lord. . . ." Theo keeps his eyes closed, never stirring. "Asleep" is what Lena says he is doing. But is anyone fooled?

Before sundown, a panhandler knocks. He's stooped under a huge backpack—so it's hard to say whether he's old or simply young and road-weary.

Something about him makes Lena uneasy. He's been here before, she could swear to it.

"Father's not available, I'm afraid."

"Not available?" It's the caller's presumption that irks Lena.

"You sure?"

"Just a minute—" Lena recalls the jar with loose change on the kitchen counter.

While she's deciding whether to empty the jar or by how much, she can hear the man tramping down the driveway, and by the time she gets to the door he's vanished.

It's then she realizes what bothered her. He was too well dressed.

She happens to know how expensive the jacket he was wearing because she'd shopped for one exactly like it for Theo's last birthday. She'd spent hours searching for something sporty yet clerically appropriate. Black, with discreet white piping, it was the only sports jacket that seemed sufficiently somber. And—it had come at no small price.

As she shuts the door it occurs to her to check the coat closet. Inside, she finds a frayed and battered over-coat, an alb and stole in pristine condition (awaiting his funeral?), and a clutter of empty wire hangers—nothing else.

* * *

IN THE EVENING, Father Kamin drops by. By then, Theo is truly, deeply asleep. Lena seizes the opportunity: "You mentioned his obsessively tidy desk," Lena begins, "how typically Germanic that is. But another story I've been hearing seems to contradict it. It's hard to follow. About a doll. Something about a doll left on the altar, desecrating the altar. . .not placed by Theo, of course, but his doing nothing to prevent it."

"Good grief! You've picked up on *that*—?" Father Kamin throws up his hands in mock horror. "Same old story still going around? It's a non-story, a non-event. I don't think his action—or inaction—was fully intended, not in the way it was taken. I'm not sure he even noticed. Most people failed to notice."

"How did it happen? Whatever did happen—" Lena wants to know.

"I didn't witness it myself," Father Kamin says. "Some people—not many, but all it takes are one or two individuals stirring things up. There are some who seem to worship all the little curtsies, the customs and costumes, the *way* we do things rather than the *What*.

"People wanting the communion rail restored, wanting the priest to turn his back on the congregation and face the altar—everything like it was in the good old days. Outright threats of bodily harm in rare cases. And there's sniping from a few of the priests themselves, chancery types, careerists, vying for advancement and the favor of the bishop. Palace intrigue—would you believe it?—in a *mission* diocese!

"I, myself, was once accused of 'making pudding on the altar.' By a member of the parish council who wanted more formality, Latin, fiddleback vestments, and such—"

"But, with the doll—you were saying? What happened?"

"Only learned of it by hearsay," Father Kamin reminds her. "It involved a far corner of the altar—a very small doll, and a three year old girl." As Lena is given to understand, the mother carried the child in her arms, the same way the child carried the doll in *her* arms. The mother received Communion, her daughter—a blessing. The daughter, wanting the same blessing for her doll, started to cry. Carried past the chalice, the child suddenly stretched her arm over her mother's shoulder and slipped the doll onto the altar. And that seemed to calm her—she stopped crying. Theo continued giving Communion and did or did not notice.

"Maybe the child was remembering the Christmas crèche," it occurs to Lena, "the baby doll in the manger."

"Yes, well, the real point, if there is any," Father Kamin reflects, "is that the doll wasn't removed at once. And it was the deacon who stepped in and picked it up."

Lena asks what Theo had to say about the incident.

"Nothing. Never said a word. He smiled, you know that smile. . . ."

She did, indeed.

"You look so much alike, the two of you. I hope you don't mind my saying."

People always said this of Theo and Lena. Long bones, prominent nose, same craggy features. On a man, they'd say it was "a strong face—full of character—a strong build, overall." With a woman, on the other hand. . . .

It's no blessing, Lena can tell you.

"There will always be complaints," Father Kamin resumes. "Unless the priest makes no waves at all—which isn't the way of the Gospel. Comforting the afflicted and afflicting the comfortable, that's our job. But, at the same time, there can be—and there is—too much trust, *blind* trust, placed in the person of the priest. We are conduits, at best, human and imperfect. A mature faith understands this."

"Theo doesn't always explain himself. He's not consistent about this. Whether it's because he thinks what he is saying is perfectly obvious, or whether he expects he'll never be understood. . .I don't know."

"The altar mishap doesn't seem to be bothering him that much, but *something's* bothering him," Lena reflects. "I keep asking: what's really eating him?"

"That's what I keep asking myself," Father Kamin says. "So many things *could* be. . . . Backbiting? But that's nothing new. Might be the weather, one of the driest years on record. It wears you out. And let's face it—we're none of us getting any younger. . . .

"But Theo was a very solid priest—prayerful, truly pastoral. There aren't many left. Only a few, really, at any time." Lena cannot fail to notice how often he speaks of Theo in past tense. "He entered minor seminary—when?—at age fourteen? We're all reckoning with choices made long ago—for Theo that must be a lifetime ago." He mentions the sisters next door, reminds her that Theo worked alongside them for decades.

"Then on top of everything else—Father Norman's death. . . . They were classmates from seminary days." Choosing to be incardinated in the same diocese, it would be only natural for Norman to become Theo's confidante or confessor. Had they'd been more than friends as far back as seminary? *Special* friends? Certain tongues might wag but Father Kamin doesn't give them much credence. Their seminary was famous for vigilance: the two of them would never have survived to ordination had this been the case; any hint of a "particular friendship" got you shipped out immediately. "The rule was inflexible: *Non quam duo, semper tres*—not in twos, always threes. . . ."

"It's an old adage: 'Two's company, three's a crowd,'" Lena is quick to chime, wanting to say something, not really thinking.

"Well, that's *sort* of the general idea, though the seminary officials were on a hunt for something insidious—quite specific. But the outcome was: you had a number of priests unable to get close to *anyone*, they were so fearful of attachment. It didn't necessarily turn their thoughts toward God.

"Norman and Theo were good friends for many, many, years—*that* much is certain." Then, just this past fall, after being diagnosed with Alzheimer's, Father Norman set off on the road to New Mexico with no maps or *GPS*, no sign of his planned destination, no indication that he had *any* plans or destination. He'd been speeding, well over the limit. The police caught up with him on the side of the road, slumped over the wheel.

"I don't think Theo's been able to grieve properly. There've been too many deaths, one after another.

"Added to that. . . ." Father Kamin alludes to recent Church scandals: "Those stories everyone's heard, some of them true, some false. Morale suffers either way. We're all affected. Not to mention everything else going on and on in the world. . . . Have we learned anything in two millennia? Has anything changed?"

"Others might be discouraged but they're not fasting to death," Lena objects. "This is different. Something's eating him from the inside."

"He has his faith to count on—that's the main thing," Father Kamin offers. He's about to say more when something stops him, his voice trails off.

Their eyes meet; lock. They stare at one another, say nothing—break away.

* * *

A DELEGATION FROM the Knights of Columbus brings over a framed certificate of appreciation.

More visitors, members of Theo's flock come to the door, but remain standing on the threshold, venturing no further. "Not wanting to disturb," they explain. They come in clusters for the most part, and when they huddle closely together for support and cast baleful eyes upon her, Lena thinks of sheep—they *look* sheepish. A few bolder ones come singly—one brings a casserole, another a special pillow. They all stop at the outer door, assuming that Theo is sleeping or praying.

Lena wonders what exactly they've been told. For her part, she can never be sure what Theo is doing in his immobility, beneath his closed lids.

"Is he. . .any better?" Sister Perpetua asks. She's come to deliver a lunch tray. Lena hasn't the heart to tell her how useless it is to persist in trying to change his mind. Sister Cecelia pokes her head in the bedroom door and chides Theo: "What? Still in bed?" If she intends to jolly him into action she has miscalculated badly. Father Kamin drops by again and starts in on the German temperament again: "It's like talking to a wall. Control! That's what his refusing to eat means— an attempt at self-deliverance. Not waiting on God's appointed time."

To the sisters, Lena promises to try and coax him back to taking more nourishment. She knows better than to promise results, but she can truthfully say that she won't give up trying. She knows there will come a point of no return when, even if Theo should want to reverse course and resume eating, his condition can no longer be reversed. They might be close to it but they are not there yet. So she continues improvising a table setting on his desk, spreading a dishtowel to cover the place where the typewriter used to sit, carefully aligning utensils right and left, and making a folded washcloth serve as a napkin. When he still refuses to come, she'll carry supper in to him, one dish at a time, prepared to feed him in bed. But after the usual altercation with the usual outcome, she'll be the one eating, to keep food from going to waste and to avoid offending the sisters who prepared it. She'll carry the tray over to the kitchen sink, not bothering to reheat any of it, and swallow with guilty haste, standing all the while.

When the time comes to retrieve the tray, Sister Perpetua brings along another sister, carrying a candle and prayer card. "He's going to a better place," they chorus.

Everyone says the same thing.

No point insisting: *There is no better place. This is our only world.* What Lena believes.

* * *

FELIPE (THE GARDENER? HANDYMAN?) brings over a folding cot, setting it down in the living room, where Lena can have a modicum of privacy. Before leaving, he pauses between the two rooms and waves to Theo. For Felipe, Theo opens his eyes.

"Promise?" he asks.

"Promise," Felipe answers.

That's it—a single word. Lena has no idea what they're talking about.

8

OUTSIDE/INSIDE

SHE HAS TO GET OUT. Unseasonable snow is predicted for the weekend—Lena expects the lines will be long. She looks forward to the bustle, though. Inside Theo's sickroom, nothing moves, the air is stifling.

Leaving the house, she is dazzled at the brightness of the day.

Once again, she considers cooking up something tempting for Theo. Again, she decides against it. She has never been much of a cook, and has no idea what, if anything, might tempt him now. The sisters who have been feeding him would be the ones to know best. And Lena's not about ready to reconstitute his kitchen—that would require a major overhaul. Taking another informal inventory, she'd found a battered iron skillet, blackened with the residue of suppers past, in a cabinet under the oven she'd not opened before. Alongside it—a half-empty cruet of oil, and a tower of plastic drinking glasses jammed one inside the other. Where could she even start?

For herself, Lena's content to boil up a couple of eggs and oatmeal. So the basics: milk, eggs, bread, cheese, some kind of fruit. . . . She doesn't need a list.

Coming back, she loses her way. Sees the strangest billboard. She could swear it says:

PAIN IS OPTIONAL
SUFFERING IS NOT

But, no, that couldn't be. Is it: *SUFFERING IS OPTIONAL, PAIN IS NOT. . .?* She doesn't think so. She might be recalling Daniel's words—"He has to stay on those sticks"—when presenting the crucifix he'd made. Maybe the Church could get away with a message promising pain or suffering to all, but what sort of medical clinic would hope to attract patients by advertising in those terms?

Back in the old days, a message like the one she thinks she read would have set Theo off, spinning and spouting. Lena could just hear him. Fact was, she *had* heard him: "People come to me for the wrong thing," he'd preached. "I can't absolve anyone from suffering. Most I can offer is a way *into* suffering, and just possibly, for anyone willing to go deep enough, a way *through*."

He'd been a little too easy with it. She wouldn't call it glib, exactly. Younger, surely.

The sign bothers her. So much so—that she circles back to find the billboard again and double-check the message. Turns out, she'd gotten it all wrong. What it says is:

> *WHEN PAIN IS* UNAVOIDABLE
> *SUFFERING IS NOT*

No homiletic fodder there, not for Christians, anyway. It's a relief, really, to be back to pragmatics. *Real life.*

* * *

BACK AT THE HOUSE, she's barely in time to reroute a prayer contingent of two, headed for Theo's bedside. Lena asks them to please pray in the living room; she isn't sure of a diplomatic way to explain to them that Father has less and less patience for words—words of any kind. "He needs to pray silently right now," is the best she can manage.

It's Sister Perpetua and she's brought along one of the laywomen who helps out with cleaning and cooking in the convent. They kneel on the bare floorboards, whip out their rosaries, and have at it.

Lena takes refuge at Theo's side. His eyes are closed but, once again, she suspects from certain small twitches and shiftings under his lids that he isn't really sleeping.

From the next room the drone of the rosary continues.

And then they start in on the *Salve Regina. . .*

". . .Mother of mercy,
Our life, our sweetness and our hope.
To you we cry,
Poor banished children of Eve,
To you we send up our sighs,
Mourning and weeping
In this valley of tears.
Turn then most gracious Advocate,
Your eyes of mercy toward us. . . ."

Suddenly his eyes open. He reaches for Lena's hand and squeezes —hard.

"After this our exile. . . ."

She is not prepared for the strength of his grasp even now. Nor for the tears in his eyes—and in her own, unbidden.

It's through something like rhyme, she thinks, *not reason, the way this seeps into you, carves a channel, takes hold. Before we understood what "mourning" meant, or "valley of tears" or "Advocate," or "exile," we learned to re-cite the words. Learned them, not by mind, but (as people say) "by heart."*

9

NIGHT AND DAY

WHAT NOW?

From the next room, Lena hears him humming. Then a metal hanger clattering to the floor. Grappling for her watch, she sees it's a few minutes past two. *Two in the morning.* Did the alarm go off?

Now a dense shadow looms above her—it's Theo standing—almost. He clutches a corner of the desk to steady himself.

When he tries to slip past her (without shoes or socks and wearing a suit jacket over his pajamas) it's too much.

"Where on earth do you think you're going?" *And where,* she wonders, *did his sudden burst of energy come from?*

"It's urgent," he explains. They are waiting on him at Fort Collins to celebrate Mass.

"I have to bring the wine and the bread."

"You're dreaming, Theo," Lena says firmly. "This can't be happening. Not at this hour. Do you have any idea what hour it is?" There was a time, growing up, when she wouldn't have hesitated telling him he was out of his mind.

"Besides," Lena reminds him, "isn't Fort Collins in Arkansas? And where are your shoes? Can't go any-place without shoes."

"Shoes?" he stares at his feet before turning. Shuf-fling back to his room, Lena hears him murmur: "Why is the parking lot so empty?"

"Because it's two in the morning." She can't help sounding as irritated as she feels.

"Let me know if you need help," she offers feebly, without budging. Theo doesn't answer but she hears him settling heavily back in bed. And he stays that way until nearly ten in the morning. She chooses not to wake him.

Let him sleep, she thinks, *and wake clear-headed. Restored. Returned to himself.* If she were able to pray, that would be her prayer, if she'd asked for a miracle—

But Lena's sleep is shattered.

When she finally falls back it feels like she's stepped into what must have been *his* dream, the one she'd not allowed him to finish. Sure enough, she's at Mass, and maybe it is Fort Collins. The church is packed, people bending, kneeling, standing, bending in unison, as though a wave washes over them. There's some sort of choral reading with the refrain "He died," then the antiphon "And we got even!"—but there's way

too much incense, a fog of incense and people cough-
ing so how can she be sure what she's hearing?

10

LAST MASS

IT'S COMING BACK TO Theo now, what happened that last Sunday.

He was exhausted to begin with. The night before, he'd tossed, wakeful for hours, fussing like a seminary student over how to tie the readings together. He told himself it would all come clear by morning—it hadn't. Then he nicked himself repeatedly while shaving. Once the Mass started, he doubted whether he'd be able to stand long enough; it was a new fear: that his legs would not support him. Somehow he must have signaled this. A chair was drawn up for him and he was grateful for it. He still can't recall exactly what he said after that. It wasn't the first time that he'd caught himself tuning in and out, listening to his own preaching as if a stranger were speaking, losing the thread. He recalled the advice he'd given one of the deacons the first time the man was permitted to preach, and worried about being "no scholar."

"Speak from your life," Theo had urged him. "Out of your own pain, speak."

But, at his last Mass, Theo found himself unable to preach from life or text. To himself, he lamented "God has grown dim to me." He would not have spoken these words aloud. But could he be sure? Living more alone than ever these days, he's often caught himself arguing with no one, talking to walls. Thought and speech—inside and outside—no longer seem so separate, the boundary between them less clear cut, ever more porous. And yet, more than a few of his parishioners seemed eager to give him a pass; asking after his health on the way out, all they claimed to have heard him say was that he wasn't feeling well. They were concerned, but not shocked or bewildered.

Once he was seated, Theo invited those who wished to come forward for anointing. It wasn't part of the day's liturgy, he wasn't confused on that score.

He was surprised when nearly all those present stepped into the aisle. They moved at an even pace, their hands stretched out to him—all but two young men in the back of the church. "He's losing it," one of them stage-whispered.

After the anointing he felt revived enough to stand and continue with the service.

Go on, he urged himself. As he began to recite the Creed, he took cover in the old formulation "*We* believe" rather than "I believe." After "light from light," he let the congregation carry him through the rest. No problem with the commingling of water and wine but, invoking the Holy Spirit at the Consecration, his voice broke and when he raised his arms he felt the Host beating like a heart before he realized that his hands were shaking. "Let us proclaim the mystery," he recited, his voice almost a whisper. He shuddered. And felt the power pass from him.

From the presider's chair, he signaled the deacon to give Communion. He summoned calm; he summoned reason. His panic was not new—it came from a much earlier time—but he'd not given way to it until now.

He closed his eyes, remembering his Mass exam at seminary, how carefully he'd copied the mapped and numbered routes for incensing the altar, and practiced liturgical bows for weeks beforehand. He worried how high he should lift the Host, where the points of his fingers should be placed, how prolonged a pause and how deeply to genuflect after the Elevation. Not expecting a high grade, but simply to pass, he prayed for steadiness—not to spill, not to scatter. Only this: *May the Lord look with kindness on this offering, may it be acceptable—may it be accepted.* The examiner, Father Bledsoe, seated front and center, would be the judge. He'd unbuckled the strap and positioned his wristwatch across the cover of the grade book in his lap—the signal to begin.

And Father Bledsoe's verdict? "Valid," yes, he thought Theo's Mass was valid. Something else about fluency coming with time, and straining less. "That wasn't the most elegant, but. . . ." Thinking back over it, his words seemed curious. How could humans, addressing God, ever be sure, ever be fluent?

And then, another thing—

Theo recalled the stranger, white-haired, bent, who'd come up to him after celebrating his first Mass on his own as a priest. A man old enough to be his grandfather who called Theo "Father." Who knelt and asked for his blessing. Barely out of his teens, the oil of ordination not yet dried on his palms, he recited the words and performed the gestures, but with an unease that's never left him.

Opening his eyes, he stared at the stained glass memorial window in the nave, depicting Saint Lawrence, one of the lesser saints in the lexicon, donated by the now-deceased widow of Samuel Lawrence. The saint, backlit by the sun at this particular moment, shone forth in green and gold. He stood before the Roman Prefect, presenting the "treasures" of his church— a motley crew of beggars and cripples clustered behind him. With one hand he held firm to the gridiron on which he would be roasted. The legend, "*assus est*" for "*roasted*" could be an error of transcription, missing the letter "*p*" for "*passus est*," the usual "*he suffered.*" Tradition, as Theo recalled, had it both ways: he suffered, then, pronouncing himself well-done on one side, asked to be turned over. What followed—Saint Lawrence becoming the patron saint of cooks—was perfectly logical. To be able to recall such minute details assured Theo that his mind was clear. Why, then, had he felt unable to preach? Simply a moment of panic?

A piercing ray from the eye of the Prefect found him out, making Theo's eyes tear. He blinked rapidly and turned his gaze on the congregation.

Although his mind had seemed crystal clear only a moment before, when Theo rose from the chair for the final blessing, the shakiness returned and he was no longer sure of anything. Clear light and shadow passed in his mind as swiftly as sun and cloud over the prairie. The shadows would return, he reminded himself, what had happened here was no momentary aberration. So he spent extra time to make sure he packed up well, taking care to bed the chalice safely in its velvet-lined casket, to tuck the paten into its silken sleeve and make doubly sure the cruets were rinsed.

* * *

Now, WAKING FROM a bad dream, his arms full of un-linked bones, Theo struggles to sit up. It is so cold! A scrim of frost whitens the sill. *Someone in the house?*

"Lena?" he calls.

She staggers in without turning on the light. He can't make out her face, there are blue shadows every-where. He has thrown off his covers. Drawing the quilt up to his chin, she pats it in place, then perches side of the bed for a moment.

Shadows again. Theo, starting to drift, catches himself; he's unwilling to re-enter the space of the dream. Though he hasn't thought of him in years, Fa-ther Bledsoe comes to mind—something else he said:

"The priest is a man who has renounced his humanity that he might be Christ for others." The theology suggested was dreadful, if not heretical. (Or was it only the phrasing?) Yet not one of the candidates for ordination had questioned him. They'd survived thus far by overlooking many things. And once in a while Bledsoe was spot-on, like the time he spoke of "the many secrets locked up in the priest's heart." Theo has forgotten the context. *Mary the mother of priests, perhaps?* Something like that. . . .

* * *

"LENA?" HE CALLS.

"Yes? Yes. What?"

"Didn't you hear me call? Why didn't you come?"

Lena does her best to explain that she's been sleeping, she needs to sleep.

"I dreamed I bought a bag of bones."

"Mmm."

Most of what he says is unintelligible to Lena, a mere droning, but here and there words come through clearly. Sometime after two a.m. he cries out "Forgive me!" so urgently she hurries to his side. Again he asks for forgiveness, but when she replies "What for?" he will not say.

A little later he announces:

"The door keeps opening no matter how many times I close it."

There's nothing wrong with the door. It closes and it locks. Every night since her arrival, Lena has been careful to lock up and to let Theo know what she's doing. But she's too tired to make a point of it right now. Right now, she needs to sleep.

She jolts to attention, though, when moments later, he asks: "*Does* God see us?" and answers himself: "Sees us—and watches over us." Lena can't help noticing how he answers himself in smaller voice, a child's voice, the singsong recitation of a child catechized by rote.

It's heartbreaking—to have journeyed so far and still be asking. His life is not—*cannot be*—an errand into nothingness. She must tell him. But she needs her sleep and, instead, she says: "You realize what time it is? We'll talk about it in the morning. In the morning."

Unconscionable! How could she forget? Mornings can no longer be taken for granted. And the next day brings no follow-up. Only broken phrases and silence.

I I

"TELL THEM I LOVE THEM"

THE FAMILY NEVER SHUNNED her after she became one of the "fallen away," but Lena always felt the distance afterwards. Though she'd left home years later than Theo and absorbed family influences that much longer, she thought of herself as the one who'd truly broken free while, in some ways, Theo never really left.

Lena still dropped in on Masses on occasion, and there'd always come that moment when people lined up to approach the altar to receive. She'd duck into the aisle so they wouldn't have to squeeze past her in the pew. Even so, one or another person would halt to let her in. Lena would decline politely, shaking her head, smiling. An instant's shuffle of regret, was there? "Even the balance trembles," she recalled—waving them on past. Then the line would move on seamlessly, ranks closed, the breach healed. Coming and going, they were likely to be singing the communion hymn "One

Bread, One Body," one of the popular modern ones she liked and once in a while she'd hum along or join in the singing. *Someday. . .maybe. . .could be. . . .* The words of the song struck her with the wistfulness of "Somewhere, Over the Rainbow"—at most, a promissory note, considering all those separated from communion, all the grains scattered, herself among them.

Yet no one seems to pay much attention when she stands aside in church nor suspect how awkward she feels meeting the members of Theo's flock as they come to his door.

They come in twos and threes usually and choose to stand on the doorstep, afraid to step inside. By now, it is generally understood that Father is going through a time of "hard testing." One couple brings a small bottle of holy water from Lourdes.

They speak gratefully of the surprise anointing they'd received at his last Mass. Although they hadn't fully understood it at the time, they see it now as his way of saying farewell and wish to thank him. They feel lost and adrift, missing their shepherd, unsure of how they'd find their way without him.

A woman, not so young herself, brings her mother in a wheelchair. Apparently Theo had anointed not only her hands, but also her face, the side paralyzed by a stroke, her face twisted up on one side. Now feeling has returned to that cheek—is it not a miracle?

Lena asks them twice if they won't step inside and tell Theo about it themselves, but they, too, are reluctant to disturb him.

"At least wait," she tells them. "I'll only be a second."

When she does tell him, using the word (*their* word) "miracle," Theo smiles. Lena guesses what he's thinking. The miracle is easily explained: No one has touched the old woman's cheek with tenderness since she became disfigured. Before—she was numb; now she could feel.

He sends Lena back with the words: "Tell them I love them."

She does as requested, all the while protesting to herself: *Not real! You can't love them all.* She has never experienced such love. In the classroom, she's cherished a few students, disliked a few, tolerated the remainder. By no stretch of the imagination, no effort of will, could she love them equally with one and the same love. Love was partial, unfair, bestowed on one and denied another. *But as for Theo's version of love?. . . Call it something else—a policy or program, an aspiration, a vision of the world-to-come should it ever come, pale cousin of what people mean when they use the word "love."*

Nevertheless, as people come to the door, he keeps on repeating these words, and Lena—what else can she do?—keeps on relaying the message. Soon, when he is no longer able to speak, he will sign the words to Lena by touching his mouth, then his heart, then pointing to the open door. And he'll top it off with an expansive sign of the cross as priests used to do on Rogation Days, casting the blessing wide over far-flung pastures.

Another "miracle" is reported. This one from the convent. A vigil candle igniting of itself in the chapel. The sisters are all aflutter. They interpret Theo's silence and apparent indifference to the news as another instance of his great humility.

* * *

IN THE EVENING when no one visits or is likely to visit, a nurse's aide comes in to change his sheets. Lena assists her as best she can. Theo shuts his eyes, shutting them out. He is rolled onto one side, the old sheet is rolled up under him, the new sheet rolled in; then turned on his other side—old sheet out, new sheet in. Theo's eyes remain closed all the while; he's not helping. Lena suspects he's awake, but by now even she can no longer be sure.

Later, turning on the news, she's convinced of it—he's awake.

She continues to need the news to be able to "orient herself in time and space" (as mental health professionals would say). To be reminded that there is a world beyond these walls.

At the tail end of the segment there's a report on an expedition to Mars planned for the near future. Funding remains the only obstacle. Thousands of people have volunteered for the mission, agreeing in advance to a one-way trip. Lena is appalled. They will never be able to leave Mars.

She had turned on the television very softly, but something overheard has caught Theo's attention. As other abilities fade, his hearing seems to become ever more acute.

Sure enough, there's a voice from the bedroom. "Turn it up!" So Lena ups the volume. It's something of a special occasion, Theo taking an interest.

But the report is soon concluded, and she can't help saying what she feels: "So sad, they'll be leaving the earth behind, never to return." It's the same sadness she feels for Theo, for the choice he's making now. Because she cannot help thinking it *is* a choice. That it doesn't have to be. Granted—he's older than those volunteer astronauts, but surely some good days, months, even years (didn't Dr. Foster grant the possibility?) still remain.

* * *

THE NEXT AFTERNOON, a new visiting nurse tries to engage Theo on the issue of food.

"Aren't you hungry?" she asks.

"Sometimes," he admits, "but less than you'd think." *Opening up to a stranger, not to me!*—Lena can't help resenting this. He even answers the follow-up question:

"Anything special we can tempt you with?"

"Nothing here," he says. It's not food he hungers for.

12

RUMMAGING

NOW, WHILE HE SLEEPS, Lena's back at that desk drawer and her search. She cannot say what exactly she is looking for but is certain she'll recognize it when she finds it. Theo's sleep is fitful at best, so she must move quickly.

She scans a letter from Luis, a prisoner who's been re-incarcerated, acknowledging Theo's disappointment, but counting on his forgiveness and faith—his own family has given up on him. He thanks Theo for the crosswords and the commissary funds for stationery and stamps. Could he help out with a little something for sneakers?

Yesterday there was a lockdown, searching for contraband. Sack lunches were thrown at the prisoners in their cells. He wanted to cry out: "We aren't animals," but kept it to himself. He's on Celexa now for anxiety and depression. They call the afternoon pill line-up "happy hour." He prays to *La Morenita*, it's better than

Celexa. *I am full of faith*, he writes, *because I've tried to live without it*. His old cellie wouldn't let him sleep; it was *"platica me"*—talk to me—all night long. Now he misses the company. His new cellie doesn't talk at all. The good thing is getting to read a lot. The chapel gives him *Saint Anthony Messenger*. He'd like a list of classics—books he should read in his lifetime. . .

The letter goes on and on for three pages (six, counting back and front, no white spaces, the words closely packed to go on one stamp). It is, Lena decides, one of the usual letters of its type, and it reveals nothing about Theo she doesn't already know.

But *this*, way to the back, looks more like it.

It's a child's composition notebook with a speckled cover and wide spaces between the lines. Seems to have been intended as a journal with entries carefully dated and daily routines accounted for. Rain gauge readings listed on the first pages. Entries starting with "Up and doing"—words all too familiar to Lena—follow. "Up and doing" is how they were raised, hearing the old proverbs. *"Wer rastet, der rostet"*—who rests, rusts. Only rarely were there words of encouragement, what others would call "positive reinforcement." Lena does remember her mother calling out *"Morgenstund hat Gold im Mund"*—the morning has gold in its mouth. Either way, though—it's taken years for Lena to learn to allow herself to linger in bed past first light, feeling guilty and unrested (though unable to go back to sleep) when she does, even today. And, apparently, it's the same with Theo.

8/17: Up after midnight. Thought I heard water hissing, that I'd left the hoses going—but it was only the wind.

8/21: Up and doing before sunup to set the hoses and start watering while the wind is down.

8/23: Hot, dry, wind up again. Pressed by parish council to lead prayers for rain.

8/24: Dry. Tired for no reason.

8/26: Up and doing—dry, dry, dry. Blowing dust. Worst drouth in 20 years. Wind will not stop. Continual thirst.

9/2: Up, up—up and doing. Dug four new traps for pocket gophers.

9/3: Norman gone. Here and gone. Found by police on road to New Mexico. He'd been speeding. Why? Trying to outrun death?

No time for goodbye. His body (I am told) was still warm.

10/15: Lost my place in the Lectionary this morning.

11/2: Cold front moving in. Frost forecast.

11/17: First killing frost.

12/3: Ice and snow. All roads in the Panhandle closed by noon. Grateful for whatever moisture, though.

12/9: Up and doing—to Mass. Bone tired.

12/10: Empty. Death ever before me. Prayer cannot pass through.

12/12: Not a voice not a whisper

1/4: The new year—what will it bring?

3/2: Terrible longing for something I have no name for—

3/7: Call it thirst.

God has grown dim to me, a priest.

Rough jottings follow. Dream fragments, hand-writing almost illegible, as if transcribed in darkness. Only one comes through clearly:

> *In a classroom. Coming in late I must stand in back. Can't see too well; the room is packed. There's a whiteboard on an easel up front, announcing the lesson for the day: A MESSAGE (is the next word FOR or FROM?). Too many heads in the way; I have to keep changing position to be sure. It's FROM THE MIND OF GOD. More writing appears, though no hand appears to write. Then I see—it's all numbers, an endless stream of numbers. They seem to be primes.*

Then—*What if this isn't a dream, but a true reading of the world?*

This would have come as no surprise to Ed, Lena reasons. The idea was familiar, if not commonplace, in his circle. The way he saw it: *If* God existed and *if* He communicated, His "word" would be spoken in numbers, and none of our usual languages. But it would have come as a shock to Theo; to him, as to most believers, this would be no word at all.

Just then she hears Theo turning. . . .

13

RESPITE

ONE OF THE HOSPICE staffers Lena has not met before calls to say he's been assigned to come over and relieve Lena that afternoon. He'll be giving Theo a bed bath and a shave—it's a good time for her to take a break.

The more reluctant Lena sounds, the more insistent he becomes: "Everyone needs a break now and then—a respite."

"Well. . . ." The opportunity is tempting to Lena. And disorienting—but it does make a certain amount of sense.

"For both your sakes," he urges. "His vital signs are stable now, so nothing's going to happen right away. The time is coming, though, and soon. You need to be rested. It's a beautiful day—grab it!"

"I guess." She has no idea where to go, what to do, how wandering without a destination might bring relief.

"Go shopping," the staffer prescribes.

Go out and buy something, you'll feel better afterward, seems to be the cultural consensus—outside the world of the cloister, that is. Where Theo lives, Lena is liable to forget. But there is nothing she needs.

It *is* a beautiful day, though, sunny and mild. Simply being out in the open air does encourage Lena to let go. She's been as tightly wound up as a clenched fist and hadn't realized.

After finding a parking spot (not a problem in these parts), she strolls aimlessly for half an hour or so, then enters the first department store to present itself.

You never know. . . . Lena picks out a cart and launches it. *Where to?* She has no idea.

These big stores seem to be the same everywhere. Round and round she goes, keeping her distance mostly, but once or twice pausing, and actually plucking out a blouse from the display rack, lifting the hanger to her chin and turning over the price tag as if she's interested, before returning it to the rack. But the price fails to register, the reason for selecting this or that particular blouse (color? style? material?) escapes her. She has blouses aplenty at home, enough clothes for the remainder of her life, and then some.

Round and round in a daydream of enticements, bright shiny bait she's not biting.

Linens and luggage, notions and hosiery. Somewhere in the thick perfumed air of beauty aids, smack dab in the middle of the aisle, she can't tolerate another minute and abandons the cart with nothing in it.

On her drive back to Theo's house, Lena picks up a radio broadcast. Half listening, mentally tuning in and out, she pricks up her ears to learn that Hugh Hefner's Playboy Mansion has gone on sale. There are no takers, and no wonder—twenty-nine bedrooms with peeling walls and moldy furniture. Plus one other detail: Hef-the-tenant comes along with the house. And of course he's not what he used to be. What with evenings spent watching old movies on television, holding the hand of his latest bunny-wife (sixty years his junior), the pair dressed in matching pajamas, clearly his revels now are ended. Bedtime at nine, according to the report, all passion spent.

* * *

IN LENA'S ABSENCE, one of the sisters from the convent has brought over yet another vial of healing water from the grotto at Lourdes. Lena is not at all sure how she's supposed to administer it. By eyedropper or syringe, as she would with other liquids? Best to wait for someone official, she decides.

Later, she overhears a rustling at the door. A pamphlet slipped through the crack underneath. She opens the door in time to spot a car backing out. Just as well: It's one of those end-time notices, could be any one of a dozen sects.

Blessings and curses, nothing out of the usual:

To those who are lost, to those who cannot find their way home. . . .

The deeper the prayer, the worse Satan will be blinded!

She doesn't have to read it through to know the proper place for it—directly into what Theo used to call his "round file," to join a few crumpled tissues. She doesn't have to ask.

Exhausted from his bed-bath, Theo sleeps through the afternoon, waking once at what should have been suppertime and once at sunset. Lena misses Ed terribly, especially now. There is no one to "tell her day to."

Lena watches the evening news. It seems to have been a day free of major calamities although, as a general rule, most news shows try to end on a lighter note. So tonight it's animal celebrities, lobsters who dance in circles, clicking their claws like castanets; one—a soloist—has been hypnotized to stand on his head. A cockatoo who recites numbers while dialing a rotary phone with his beak and waits for a voice before greeting "What's up?" Lena catches herself nodding.

And so to bed, all passion spent.

* * *

IN THE ONLY DREAM she can remember, Lena finds herself at a giant rummage sale. It's huge, a warehouse full. Making her way from rack to rack she recognizes a whole row of dresses, her own castoffs from years gone by. She'd completely forgotten the blue dress with the white lace collar, and all the blouses, skirts, belts, and scarves that were once hers—they're all here. So many? She doesn't want to buy anything back, she's not in the least interested. She hadn't noticed the dust before, but now she notices, the place is thick with dust. All she wants is *out of there—fast!* But—soon as she starts heading for the exit—she hears the rustling of cloth, the jostle of wire hangers, the grinding of rack wheels gaining on her. She turns: sees platoons, rack on rack, clanging, colliding, coming at her. She starts to run. Something metal nips her heel—

Waking, Lena shudders, and the words "*as terrible as an army with banners*" come to mind.

Only a dream. Her dread is completely absurd.

Unrested, but grateful to find herself whole, intact, socketed in place and in her right mind, Lena turns to face the day.

14

REMEMBERING

TODAY, LENA CAN'T forget, is the ten-month anniversary of Ed's death.

He'd seemed healthy enough over the years, had never been a smoker, had exercised regularly, but then, out of the blue, X-rays showed something unexpected. Lung cancer. It turned out to be Stage 4—a lifespan of months, at best.

Ed was stoic about his sentence. Now and then he grumbled, "What a bummer!" But he never tried to bargain with death, never asked "why me?" Instead, he made a point of insisting: "Why *not me?* It was bound to be something or other" and "I've had a good run." He had no wish for an afterlife. For Lena's sake, he'd endured chemo and radiation, buying a little more time. When both of them agreed that the extra days weren't worth it, he'd opted for palliative care and "quality of life." Then continued calm (outwardly, at least) and clear-minded until the evening before it happened. On a self-regulated morphine drip for most of the week, he'd not used it fully until the very end.

Calmly awaiting extinction? It's still hard for Lena to credit that such a thing could be—*had* been—accomplished. But she'd been a witness.

Only one troubling moment—an aberration, surely—when he asked: "Who was I?"

His voice was frail and far away, yet somehow piercing; she hadn't misheard. But she did not dwell on his peculiar phrasing of the question, which, thankfully, was never repeated. *A moment, that's all.*

He was high on morphine by then and near the end.

There'd been a memorial service, a gathering of friends and colleagues at the school where he'd taught. Instead of quotations from scripture there'd been a full-throated invocation of Bertrand Russell's manifesto "A Free Man's Worship," as orotund as any sermon. Not so different there. But its message that humans, along with the rest of the earth's inhabitants, came into being without prevision or purpose and would disappear in the "debris of a universe in ruins" was far from standard fare.

Weeks before, Ed himself had planned his memorial in detail. "No pablum, please!" By refusing to offer false comfort, he meant it to be bracing—liberating. And it did seem to give heart to others present, although it didn't work quite that way for Lena.

Lena had not informed the rest of the family and even postponed telling Theo until the few formalities

that passed for a funeral were concluded. Theo had
answered with phone calls and letters, sounding genu-
inely commiserative without being preachy. He must
have passed on the news to Frank, though, and the
expected followed: prayers, Mass intentions, heartfelt
condolences. . . .

They, too, meant well.

Inevitably, the aftermath of Ed's funeral brought
back the days that followed Theo's departure for seminary. It marked the end of childhood for Lena, yet she
was still a child. She'd taken her first steps into Theo's
outstretched arms. It was Theo who'd taught her to
read, sensing her hunger and readiness long before she
started school, when he'd caught her standing over his
shoulder trying to mouth the words he was reading.
Her mother, busy in kitchen and out in the fields and
with younger children, never had the time to spare or
even notice.

In her desolation, Lena's first recourse had been
to piety. Strict observance of the Church calendar, the
fasts, feasts, and holy days of obligation were no longer
enough for her. At a parish rummage sale she'd found
a well-worn Book of Hours, a lay version of the Di-
vine Office that (she assumed) now ruled Theo's hours.
She could never keep the canonical hours of course.
Still, reading the Office, even in an abbreviated version,
even piecemeal, promised a way of keeping in touch
with him, with what she imagined his life to be. All
she could do was imagine, since the family couldn't

afford to visit, and his infrequent letters, combed over by seminary officials, never said much.

It was a clumsy attempt at mimicry; and, rushing through the prayers as she did, provided no healing. But for the first few months she threw herself into the effort. It was all effort. School and chores kept interrupting, though that wasn't the problem. She was angry: Theo's departure (desertion, as she felt it for many months) was a deep wound. Then, slowly, her anger became something else—a determination to follow Theo's example—to pick up and leave. He proved it could be done. She knew it would harder for a girl; it would take years more time, but her resolve had hardened. However long it took, she was prepared to wait. She made no waves. She was in the family, the parish, the school, the village, but not of them. The people around her still spoke of Catholics who left the Church as "fallen away," but the process was nowhere near that dramatic. Simply—gradually—she'd become unstitched from the faith. Faith, she decided, was more a matter of belonging than signing on to this or that belief, and she did not belong.

As it turned out, it took eight, nearly nine long years, keeping her own counsel, finishing high school, then working and saving up until she could afford to strike out for the big city. But then, unlike now, there'd been a future beckoning.

* * *

HER MANNERS ARE non-existent. Lena stands over the sink, gobbling without tasting the chicken and English peas from the tray the sisters have prepared for Theo but which he refuses even to look at. She takes big hurried bites, feeling guilty for eating at all.

"Tell them my doctor prohibited. Prohibited!" Theo orders (with what seriousness she can't tell) as he pushes the tray away.

She'll tell them nothing of the kind. Feelings would be hurt. It occurs to Lena belatedly that Sister Perpetua may have guessed the true state of affairs all along, ever since she offered to send over two trays and Lena—thanking her for the offer—refused, saying she'd take care of her own meals. Ever since then, the single tray has contained more than enough food for one adult.

Sister Perpetua carries the tray herself, a passport of sorts; Lena gets this. When she lingers, Lena understands that she wants to pray a rosary while she's here, but not to disturb Theo's nap and offers her the living room with what chairs remain. If, as it turns out, she prefers to kneel on the bare floorboards, she's more than welcome to it.

When sister leaves, Lena notices little things left behind, seemingly forgotten but clearly items carefully considered, purposefully smuggled in: a saint's medal, a holy card with rainbow-colored rays emanating from the exposed heart of Jesus. A scapular of Our Lady of Mount Carmel promising him the gift of perseverance, of which he has no lack. Less, right now, would be an improvement in Lena's view. When she carries these offerings to Theo's bedside, he waves them away and points in the direction of his catchall—his desk. She stashes them in one of the empty middle drawers.

To all intents and purposes Theo has stopped eating. Lena still hasn't given up urging, going through the motions of setting the table by spreading a dishtowel on top of his desk at normal eating times and inviting him to come. When he refuses to rise, she offers to bring the tray to him in bed. But it's no go, either way.

And, really, isn't it for her own sake that she does this, so that she'll have left nothing undone?

Why am I here? Lena keeps asking herself. What did the diocese have in mind in approving Theo's request and calling her to his side? To witness? To dissuade him? To soften—or hasten—his dying? She cannot answer for the powers that be—only for herself:

I'm here because I would not choose to be anywhere else.

As Theo sleeps, or pretends to sleep. Lena spends more and more of the time standing at the kitchen window. She has taken to brushing her teeth leaning over the sink there. Theo's bathroom mirror is too intimate, she feels trapped in the same frame as Theo, her face—his face, the resemblance between the two of them ever more unmistakable.

Here, now, standing at her post by the kitchen window, Lena marvels at what she is seeing. *Hard to believe, on the very cusp of Spring. . . .*

Floating down slowly, settling gently as if in bene-
diction, snow feathers the glass, casts its thin gauze
over the sill and dampens the bird feeder which Felipe
has kept full. But no birds come.

15

QUICK SPIN

AFTER THAT BRIEF snow flurry the evening before, the next morning seems positively balmy, a foretaste of changes to come. While Theo naps, Lena steps outside for a breath of fresh air, a quick spin around the garden.

Nothing doing in the flowerbed, or, at least—nothing visible above ground. It looks like a bone yard: withered stalks and brown leaves for the most part, a few green weeds. Then she notices the tags, laminated, carefully printed, and stoops to read them: *Lamplighter, Sage, Sailing On, Red Sedum, Flaming Poppa, Beckoning Tiger, Sea Glass—*

Flaming Poppa. And—Sea Glass?

She's never seen flowers with names like these. *Did he make them up?*

She wouldn't put it past him.

Feather Down. Fooled Me (a private joke?). *Lifted Hands.*

Lena doesn't dare stay outside longer. For one thing, she's afraid the phone might start ringing and Theo, who seems increasingly sensitive to sounds, attempt to haul himself out of bed to answer it, stumbling and falling in the process. He seems weaker with each passing day.

Someone called last night but hung up immediately on hearing Lena's voice. Late in the night, when the phone rang again, she could swear it was the same caller.

"Can I speak to Father?"

Probably someone Theo had been counseling. Lena had often teased him about "acting as a poor man's psychiatrist—and with what credentials?" Anyone calling at this hour was probably desperate, in need of professional help.

"You want to give me your name and number—and a message?" Lena prompted.

"It's useless," the caller said.

"Just a sec." Lena put the phone down to retrieve Father Kamin's number (left there for just this circumstance) from the other room. She picked it up again in time to catch the click of disconnection.

Perhaps he'd call back.

He did. This would make it the third time, and, this time, he explained:

"I'm sitting here with my dog on my lap. I'm putting him down, see."

What do you say to this?

"Hello? Hello. . .you there?"

"Don't hang up. My dog is dying! I'm putting him to sleep on my lap."

Nothing to do but try and wing it. "Where are you calling from?"—hardly a promising start. He said something mushy in reply, sounded like nothing she'd ever heard of—and she said "*What?*"

"Muleshoe!" he insisted. "Mule *shoe!*"

"Spell it!" she replied.

They went on like that—it was crazy—but it scarcely mattered what Lena said or whether she said anything at all. Every now and then he'd ask: "You still there?" and she'd murmur: "I'm here." All he seemed to need was the reassurance of a receiving ear. Muleshoe, she learned, was the name of an actual town in Bailey County, not far from here. The dog's name was "Jimmy" and he was "every bit a person—more so than most people." They'd been best buddies for twelve years. When he'd settled Jimmy on his lap for the last time, the dog had licked his hand. Whenever Lena paused, wondering what to say, he repeated: "You still there? Don't hang up. Please. He's breathing hard."

Then, after a long pause: "His fur's wet—he's gone heavy now—Jimmy's gone. Nobody here, only me."

Sleep was out of the question for Lena by then. She'd done her part and let him talk himself out. The strange thing was, she never caught the man's name and couldn't recall whether he'd ever mentioned it. She knew the name of his dog, but he'd remain simply "the man from Muleshoe" should she happen to think of him again.

When he said finally, "Tell Father Theo I called—"
Lena said nothing to suggest otherwise—*what would
be the point?*

* * *

THEO WAS STIRRING. Lena heard him take a big bite of
air, his teeth clashing.

"Where you been?" he greeted her.

"Right here. Just stepped into the other room for
a sec—"

"You *look* like Lena," he said. No trace of a smile,
but Lena chose to believe that he was only teasing.

"I *am* Lena," she answered.

"Well, stay. *Be* with me."

"I *am* with you," she said. "Can you feel my hand?"

With eyes open he was fumbling in the air for her
hand. "I am not afraid," he whispered.

"Never said you were," she assured him. She could
feel his heart pounding.

He's been having one dream after another, he tells
her. In one, the phone would not stop ringing; then he's
driving, speeding, when the steering wheel comes off
in his hands. He closes his eyes while still driving. . . .

In another he's digging in Uncle Albert's field
(Frank's field afterwards), trying to find a mason jar
he'd buried there. In the dream—but he wonders now:
was it only a dream?—he's completely lost. The fence
posts have been moved, the field divided, there is no
marker.

"Sort of like a time capsule?" Lena asks. "You think you really *did* this? Buried the jar, and tried to dig it up decades later?" She has no recollection of any such thing. Was she ever part of either project? She asks what he put in the jar.

"Stuff. . . ." He frowned, struggling to recapture it. "Treasure. . .kid treasure. Arrowheads. Marbles."

Another morning comes. Another afternoon. Theo sleeps, wakes briefly, raises one hand to the light.

Light spills through his fingers. Like sand. . . .

In his dream he'd been beach-combing. Norman was with him. Everything shone, the sun-burnished sand, a sapphire sea—

Yet another dream had been comforting, but he could not remember what it was.

16

WORDS

WHILE THEO SLEEPS, LENA is back at his desk drawer, sorting through loose notes, still in search of an explanation. Not everything is legible.

There's a comment on a certain Father Sullivan who cannot sleep for worry about mice breaking and entering the tabernacle, devouring the consecrated Hosts reserved within and leaving a trail of crumbs, *each crumb containing the entire body of Christ. As we were taught,* Theo writes, and adds: *as they are still taught.*

At his funeral, the word was: "His faith is known to God alone." And Theo asks: *What will they say about me?*

Then his resolve: *Make a list / call it WHAT I STILL BELIEVE.*

A small cough from the bedroom and the drawer is shut. He's too restless for Lena to continue tonight.

* * *

Waking at first light. Theo is restless, his hands wander, pause a moment between his legs—*still there*—resume wandering.

Andy, a visiting hospice nurse, arrives before nine to bathe and turn Theo. He leaves behind a small arsenal of medications:

> Lorazepam for anxiety. (To take the edge off things, but not enough to zonk him out.)
> Morphine
> Syringes for morphine 0.2 ml
> Artificial tears for dry eyes
> Syringe for water into mouth
> Lanolin for cracked lips
> Suppositories

Andy says his heart is beating fast: "Won't be long now."

Brushing away invisible ants, plucking at the quilt, swiping his forefinger over it—back and forth—as though reading by finger-light, all these are signs.

The morning is hectic. Felipe visits. Sister Perpetua, Fathers Ryan and Kamin, all drop in briefly. Another hospice nurse appears. She too notices Theo's hands. "He's playing harps already," she says.

Someone—whether by accident or on purpose—has detached the phone; it's just as well.

* * *

Tower bells trouble the air. It's the Angelus.

Theo thinks of that jar he buried so long ago. The one time he'd been able to afford a visit home from seminary, he meant to find it—but the landmark he'd chosen (a fencepost, of all dumb things) had been moved, he didn't know where to start.

Even at the time he recognized it as a time capsule and his farewell to childhood.

No idea of its whereabouts, but now he recalls exactly what he chose to place inside. He's unpacking his treasures: a bucking bronco he'd fashioned from horseshoe nails. . .a couple of arrowheads. . .a purplish geode split to show the white crystals nested inside, crystals he once called "jewels" and, in childish innocence, believed they were. What else? Bunch of marbles, swirlies, aggies, cats eyes. . . . He should've written a letter to his descendant—himself—*Then* to *Now*.

* * *

AFTERNOON. LENA HAS moved her cot into Theo's bedroom, alongside his bed. That way, she can attend to him without hopping up and down all night.

She rarely quits his side now. His eyes are open, pupils wide, as if to fathom darkness. She leaves a small nightlight going, but that's not what keeps him awake. The nightlight is in the bathroom over the sink, out of his angle of vision.

Before dawn, he cries out, something about a bad dream. "Trying to get across. . . ."

He is not dreaming now, but all too fully awake, reliving the memory of that Christmas night barely over a year ago. A night of pitch blackness, delirium, the heat intolerable. Sick with fever but doesn't know it, he thinks it's the furnace and needs help to turn it down. He doesn't want to call Felipe, interrupting his precious family time. Nor does he want to wake the sisters.

With lights out in the convent (and no star in the east to guide him), without a pinprick of light to pierce the darkness overhead, he turns towards a faint cluster of house lights in the distance. How he wishes he'd taken a flashlight! But he hasn't planned, simply acted—reacted.

Blindly he plunges on.

And now where? Everything's shifted. The row of house lights he struggled to keep in his sights now stands more to his side than ahead of him and no closer than when he started out; he's made no forward progress.

It's bitter burning cold; his slippers are sodden, no socks, no jacket. A dog—white, or covered in snow— materializes out of the darkness, rushes up, nuzzles his ankles, sniffs his crotch.

"Git!" Theo cries—in his father's voice. "Now's no time to play!" The dog halts, listens, but then abruptly turns away, bounds off, rump in the air.

"No—No! Come back," he calls after him. "Lead the way." Too late—

He's zigzagging—doubling back on himself. Stumbling over a stone, he recovers, then a patch of stubble buried in snow throws him to his knees. His feet feel nothing; fingers left him long ago. Nothing he can do but plunge deeper into the dark.

What he's aiming at are lights from Christmas trees in living rooms. *Warmth, welcome, rest. . . . Kindness*—all he asks. But those lights remain chambered, illumine no path through the blackness of the night.

By the time he picks up faint tinny sounds, a thread—it's Jingle Bells—he is shaking with cold. He's forgotten why he ever stepped outside.

Coming up to the houses at last, only one door opens to him, and only partway. The woman does not recognize him. There's a tree with lights behind her. He doesn't recognize her—her face, backlit, is blotted out. The door shuts, a lock clicks.

Another door. Does not open. The next. A corner of the blind lifts: a child's face peeks out, flattens against the glass. Someone must be calling the police. When the patrol car swerves towards him and comes right up over the curb, he is only too happy to step inside.

* * *

LAST VISIT, SISTER PERPETUA pronounced: "He's ready to go. But the Lord's not ready to take him yet."

This morning, hesitant, she knocks three times before entering. "Come on in!" Lena calls. "The door is open—unlocked, as usual." Sister Perpetua slips quietly into the room and positions herself across from Lena on the opposite side of the bed.

Suddenly Theo speaks out. They lean in to listen, but it's all over so quickly. Before they know what's happened, he is done speaking. Silence resumes.

What if these were to be his last words?

Pausing at the outer door as sister prepares to leave, Lena asks her whether she could make out what Theo was trying to say.

"Of course!" she smiles. "He said 'Jesus.' Like this—'Je-*sus*!' He called on the name of our Lord." She's been waiting for Theo's last words, anticipating them. Lena doesn't doubt for a moment that she heard what she says she's heard. It makes perfect sense. For Lena, though, there is no such certainty, no clarity. He might have been saying "see this" or "sees us." It might have been "sea glass," it's possible. Two breaths: a rising, a falling, the word—or words—drowned in sibilance, his speech so wheezy and blurred.

17

READING THE DARK

HE HEARS RAIN. It does not answer his thirst. His palate is sculpted like a seabed, his tongue cleaves to it—his mouth is so parched.

His finger continues to move back and forth across the quilt, reading in the dark. Reading the dark. Then his hand falls away.

Sleep falls like rain on the roof of the house.

In his dream, Lena is driving. They have found the restaurant at last. It's crowded, confusing—there are too many people, too many choices. He craves water but as soon as the glass is set down before him it is snatched away. The menu is tacked to the wall but the names of the dishes are bitten off. One by one, small bowls of food are set before him. He names each food as it comes: fish, string beans, corn, pudding. Once named, the item vanishes. Someone is striking his forehead with a serving spoon. *Must go, no time to sit, must leave right away.* Outside—people are stripping the leaves from the trees and eating them. He wakes briefly, it's raining. *The rain is for real.* Sounds like a cat's tongue scraping a dry bowl.

Lena dreams she is holding a chest X-ray. She holds it high up to the light and stares into the bell-shaped chest cavity at cloud, cobweb, mist—Ed is dissolving before her eyes. . . . And now she faces a waterfall. She is one of a crowd standing at the base of a giant stone face. Reverence is being paid. Gathered on a scaffold overhead, priests in long robes anoint the great head with milk poured from their pitchers. A body is hurled from the scaffold. Does anyone notice? Lena weeps as milk streams over the stone forehead, the wide-open eyes, the wings of the nose, the phil-trum, the slightly parted lips.

The great eyes are blank, they do not blink. . . .

Theo dreams the bishop is spraying his yard with weed killer. Father Kamin is inside, vacuuming and smoking a cigarette, tapping the long ash into his palm. Ash cascades to the floor. Lena sits on the edge of her cot. She is busy weeping. His own bed is empty—is it over, then?

His grand-nephew Daniel enters the house sing-ing, he has brought a dog along. . . .

Rain continues to fall. Here and there (because of the rain?) their dreams mesh.

Lena is driving through a downpour, lights murky, wipers hissing on and off, no help at all. She must get the house ready. But first she must find the house. *Is it here?* The trees are leafless, blackened with damp. Patches of white flicker like moths between the branches. Coming closer, she sees the branches are draped with towels and sheets, all sodden, dripping. . . . *Is this the place?*

Theo dreams he is standing at the door of his house. The wind is up. He's chilled through and through. The door is locked; he pounds—uselessly. From inside he hears Lena scold in his mother's voice: "No time for play—come inside!"

Why doesn't she hear him? He ransacks his pockets for the key he does not carry. . . .

Lena struggles to open her eyes. *Not yet day!* She draws the blanket up to her chin, hoping to fall back to sleep, to recapture and complete her dream. To *resolve* her dream, if such a thing were possible. She's still looking for (a house? a place? a country?) she's supposed to recognize, but cannot find. The house she wakes in is unfamiliar, damp and cold. This isn't it. Then someone—something—shakes her awake, calls her by name. For a moment she imagines it's Theo asking, "What's for dessert?" but quickly she corrects herself—*How I wish.* . . . It couldn't be Theo, who seems to be sleeping deeply. Lena wonders what he's been dreaming. *Does he still dream?*

Is it the rain she hears, or something—someone— moving *inside* the house?

Maybe check the gas stove? She's pretty sure she checked (an old habit) before settling down for the night, but it doesn't hurt to be doubly sure.

She finds the pilot light on and all the burners operational.

Here it is! Theo, still wrapped in his dream, plucks the key from its hiding place inside his ear. Then plucks his ear from the side of his face. Wherever he looks, leaves are whirling.

Then he's awake, but only in the dream.

Why is she standing here? Lena stalls in the doorway of the unlighted kitchen—clueless. Most likely one of those "senior moments" happening with increasing frequency lately. She thinks she's in the right place but how can she be sure, the object of her search lost to her, wiped with darkness?

She wanders from kitchen to bedroom and back. The house is so small it can't really be called "wandering," though; "pacing" is more like it.

She hears Theo murmur: "What do I do now?"

Theo opens his eyes to darkness, not knowing how long he has slept. But—*was it sleep?*

Is this waking, then?

Rain crackles on the roof.

18

OUTWARD AND VISIBLE SIGNS

HE'S ON HIS KNEES—in his garden. Dreaming and waking, flickering between them. Lena, exhausted, perching on the bed beside him, leans against the headboard.

Theo takes her hand and folds it in both his own. There have been no more words from him since Sister Perpetua's last visit. No more *spoken* words—but he's definitely gesturing towards someone or something, gesturing with intent and exact replication, over and over. Some kind of hand-speak. Bewildered at first, Lena comes to realize that what he is doing is giving Communion.

His hand mimes the old gestures. Repeatedly, he plucks something from the sheet, raising, and resting it an instant in midair, then into the joined hands of someone standing before him with the gesture of placing a gold coin or gem—something rare and precious—into a cup. Lena knows he's seeing the distinct faces of individuals because every now and then he extends only his fingertips to place the Host the old-fashioned way, into the open mouth of the person standing before him.

No question: he sees them. Hand. Mouth. Hand. Hand. Mouth—recalling individual custom—and he thumbs the sign of the cross onto the forehead of what must be a child carried in a woman's arms.

Feed my flock. Starving, himself, he keeps on dishing it out.

* * *

IN AND OUT OF dreams. . . .

Theo cannot receive Communion, cannot swallow even a tiny fragment of the Host. Last time someone tried, he coughed and coughed, almost choked.

You'd think that now at last, he'd allow himself some well-earned rest. But no, not a bit, he's never still. Lena can't get through to him. She strokes his shoulder to soothe him. His hand wanders the sheets, but no longer seeks her hand.

Pray, Lena urges herself. *Pray as though someone somewhere were listening and might even wave.* It doesn't work. Instead, she stands at the front door, staring out at Theo's winter garden. The fresh air is welcome; it seems a pity to smoke as she's about to do. She quit for good two years back and mostly stuck to it; only when severely stressed does she allow herself to light up. It's not really a nicotine craving, but something more subtle: the need to see her own breath, breath being an outward and visible sign of spirit, if not the thing itself. She exhales—visibly—to convince herself that she's still alive.

But she only takes three quick puffs before returning bedside.

He's very near.

Does he recognize Lena? His eyes are open wide, but it's unclear what he sees, or that he sees at all. Sister Perpetua calls it "angel gazing"—he's already turned away from this world. "He's on his way."

The bishop comes to anoint Theo.

The vicar general follows within the hour. He prays on behalf of Theo who remains perfectly silent:

> "Have mercy on me, O God,
> according to Your great mercy,
> and according to the multitude
> of Your tender mercies,
> blot out my iniquity. . . ."

Theo's praying (if that's what he's doing) is wordless, unclamoring, whether wanting or wishing, repenting or fearing, there's no way for Lena to tell.

While the vicar "happens to be here," he wonders whether it might be a suitable moment to pick up the vestments Theo requested for the funeral.

Lena opens the coat closet. There can be no ambiguity about Theo's intentions: they're (literally) black and white. The worn black overcoat, clearly destined for charity, and his alb, draped with a plain white stole.

"Oh, wait—" On impulse, she dashes back to the bedroom to fetch Daniel's crucifix, still on the bedside table. She tells herself this is not a betrayal: Theo has kept it with him through his travail. He'd gotten rid of everything that might be considered "religious paraphernalia" but permitted this.

"What *is* this?" The vicar frowns with displeasure, turning the crudely-made crucifix over in his hand before pocketing it. "A nicer stole, at least," he fumes, not quite under his breath: "He might have allowed himself. . .he wasn't a Carthusian, or a Quaker, for heaven's sake. . . ." But, having had his say, he lets the matter pass: "All set, I guess." He carries the alb by its hanger, lifting it high so as not to crease it or soil the hem.

* * *

THEO IS COLD, is fevered. He sweats. He shivers. Dying is hard work. His kidneys are failing. Over and over, Lena dips the little sponge in a glass of water and swabs his parched lips.

His breathing is labored. Sounds like someone knocking at a door. Then. . .the door is taken away. It's quiet.

How quiet it is.

19

NIGHT

ONCE THE PROFESSIONALS take over, everything seems to happen at once. The vicar general enters—then a nurse to confiscate the remaining drugs,
anxious that each drop of morphine be accounted for.
Word has gone out; the sisters must have been waiting in the wings: Sisters Perpetua, Dorothy, Dymphna,
Hildegard, Sixtus, and Cecelia, even Josepha in her
wheelchair, crowd every inch of space in Father Theo's
tiny house. Only minutes later, two staffers from the
funeral home arrive, wheeling a gurney. They banish
everyone from the bedroom and proceed to do whatever they are doing behind a shut door.

Waiting for the door to open, the sisters reach for
their rosaries.

They form a line to witness the gurney's passage
from the bedroom, through the living room and out
the front door. The gurney is covered by a blue blanket;
under it: a mound—of something, it might have been

anything, a pile of folded blankets, nothing human, surely not Father Theo, himself. The sisters reach out to touch the covering blanket for whatever trace or connection remains, bless themselves, and weep.

Lena can do nothing but look on, dry-eyed, hands lifeless at her side; she has no way of externalizing what she is feeling.

Or perhaps she is no longer feeling?

Late in the afternoon, she receives a call informing her that he is "done."

"Done?" she echoes.

It must be a trainee, new to the niceties.

"Ready for viewing. Coffin-ready," he blurts.

The wake and the funeral will follow shortly.

Lena busies herself with the laundry, stripping Theo's mattress, folding clean sheets and pillowcases and stacking them on top of the dryer. And then— there is nothing more for her to do.

When Sister Perpetua brings over a dinner tray, this one unmistakably designated for her, Lena does her best to at least taste everything on the tray, although she has no appetite. The sisters urge her to sleep over at the convent or have one of them stay over at the house with her. Lena thanks them but begs off, saying she needs to get used to solitary time, and they do not insist.

* * *

NIGHT

THE NIGHT IS LONG, borderless. Death is never far from her mind. She recalls telling Ed, "I want to go in my sleep" and remains convinced that the best way, the best of the bad, is to slip into sleep and, by imperceptible transitions, into oblivion. Wake me up when it's all over would be her preference. Ed, on the contrary, wanted to die with full consciousness and perhaps he did, he never told. He *seemed* to be awake, as Theo seemed to be. No use pursuing this—they've packed their secrets in and taken them with them.

She's free now to explore the notes he'd left in the desk drawer; and, early in the morning, still muggy for want of sleep, she returns to rummaging and her interrupted reading of the notebook with the speckled cover.

My feet drag, the errand is urgent. . . . An empty lot. . . . A high overpass. . . . A classroom, a whiteboard. . . . God speaking in numbers. . . . She's seen this before.

She'll carry the notebook back home with her and read through it slowly. She won't ask for permission; she doesn't think of it as stealing. She's simply claiming what belongs to her—her portion of inheritance. And who else would want it, really? It's doubtful she'll be challenged, doubtful that anyone else knew the notebook existed.

While she's at it, she gathers all the loose scraps, including his notes on the weather, and tucks them inside the notebook. *For another day. . . .*

Her suitcase is stashed in the front closet. Nothing else remaining there now that Theo's vestments are gone—only that worn overcoat, a few empty hangers. Lena, herself, is packed, though still unready to leave— unready for Theo to leave—still arguing with him. And she catches herself clutching the sleeve of his overcoat as if that might detain him.

* * *

LENA STRETCHES OUT in the recliner, the "kick-back chair" she slept in during her first nights at the house. The television screen in front of her is blank and will remain so. For hours on end, she stares into darkness, unwilling to turn on a lamp.

The house is full of echoes, though—an intermittent mumble. If they *are* words, she can't make them out. Who speaks? Voices come out of the walls.

It must be the wind.

20

AFTER

TOWARDS MORNING SHE SLEEPS—an hour or two maybe—then startles awake, so convinced that Theo has just whispered, "If you'd let me finish" that she whispers back, "I'm listening." But, of course, no one has spoken, the house is empty. She's alone.

It is still dark.

* * *

DAYBREAK: THE GRUMBLE of cars starting up in the morning chill. Soon—elsewhere—the new day will be greeted with the thump of the morning paper on doorsteps, with bowls and steaming cups, the clatter of spoons. With voices answering voices.

Soon, too, Lena will be returning to her apartment, entering a city grown newly strange. Everybody so busy. For the first time in her life she will be entirely free. There will be nothing she *has* to do. Nothing she is expected to do. Already it begins, she feels it. The unaccustomed leisure will weigh upon her; she will not welcome it, or call it "freedom."

Her apartment, too long closed in on itself, will be musty. Before unpacking, she'll crack open the windows to let in air, along with the toxins of the city. Shouts and greetings will rise from the street, none addressed to her. Perhaps she'll nod to the elderly woman at the window of the apartment house facing hers, a watcher of the street, who for years has seemed to be planted there, head in hands, elbows propped on the sill. But most likely the old woman will be gone now.

Will I become a face in the window? Lena wonders. *One of those leftover women? All alone. . . .* She recognizes the mood, the swell of self-pity, and checks herself: *Don't even start. For who is not alone? Think of the man from Muleshoe. Think of Theo, alone in the midst of many—*

And today belongs to Theo.

* * *

LAST NIGHT'S WIND has subsided. Skies today will be clear, the weatherman promises. Lena tips the blind to see for herself. Despite the haze of new leaves on the trees and shoots of green grass among the sere, it's not what you'd call nice weather. The sky shines with a hard, mineral, brightness.

"Severe clear," the weatherman calls it.

Theo's cupboard is down to bare boards—literally. Only a few teaspoons of instant coffee in a jar remain— enough for Lena's wake-up cup of black coffee, anyway.

Lena has not yet wept. Squeezed dry, how she feels.

Frank's family foregathers in Theo's living room. The rest have already gone on ahead to the church. The men stand, and Lena stands. There aren't enough places for everyone to sit and, anyway, they won't be staying.

They say the words people always say.

Only Frank dares a note of disharmony. Speaking for himself, he confesses that he's not entirely at peace with Theo's decision to be buried away from his birth-place. He's trying—doing his best to accept it. This is the place where Theo has served; he understands. And yet—

Again he asks Lena: Isn't there something here that she wants? How about the kickback chair? The bird feeder—?

—Nothing?

There is nothing she wants, aside from the note-book and papers she doesn't mention and has already packed away.

Daniel has not been allowed to bring his dog with him. The child moves restlessly back and forth, stoop-ing under the desk, hunting under the bed, scratching around in bureau drawers, opening closet doors, in search of the person for whose sake they have come. Who must be hiding somewhere in the house. As he searches, he chants "I spy with my little eye" over and over. It's quite irritating, impossible to ignore—like an earworm. He must think Theo's disappearance is a game. On his knees he stirs up the dust, retrieving a stray button and an orphan shoe from under the bed and, from the deep recesses of the bedroom closet, a confessional stole. These are the only traces left. The stole is dark purple, narrow as a ribbon, easy enough to have missed in the shadows.

* * *

THE CHURCH FUNERAL is brisk. Members of the family in the lead are hustled down the center aisle, pressed forward by the priests following them, propelled in turn by the bishop at the end of the line.

There are many prayer petitions to the Lord offered on Theo's behalf, mostly rote. Lena lets them pass over her. But the words "true and faithful servant"—coming from the mouth of the bishop and considering the turmoil of Theo's recent weeks—summon her full attention. Lena silently amens them. *Faithful, yes. . . .* Amens, and amends them: *True—truer than you know.*

"No longer servant, but friend," Father Kamin begins. "Shortly before his death, when he could no longer speak, he sang. In silence—but, from the way his lips moved, the way his breaths were spaced, I could tell he was singing—and you'll be glad to know that he was no longer off-key!" (Pausing for a little levity here.)

Then, with entire seriousness, he resumes: "When he could no longer pray, his hands continued to bless."

It was so, Lena has to admit.

* * *

TIME FOR THE RITE of committal, the final farewell.

It's bright out, if cold, the sky a vacancy: unblemished blue, without a wisp of cloud. ("Severe clear" exactly as the weatherman said it would be.) Their small procession—all but Frank and Daniel—pass through the cemetery gate in silence.

Daniel, who's been so quiet and well-behaved in church, now balks, refuses to pass though. He wraps both hands around one of the iron spears of the fence and clings for dear life. Words are useless. He will not budge. Not wanting to create a scene by resorting to force, Frank waves Lena and the others on. They'd best start without him.

Off to the side a backhoe awaits, arm and scoop cocked in readiness, a huge mound of fill-dirt alongside it. A smaller mound of ceremonial fill waits at grave's edge where Lena and the other mourners gather.

The grave is narrow, dark and deep. Lena stares into the pit. *Perpetual light shine upon him.* . . . She stoops to palm a handful of earth. It crumbles to a fine dust, scatters to air—it is so dry.

"Digging a place for him, we found no stones," Felipe whispers. "All the way down—not one stone! A miracle." Words intended as a salve. He is doing his best to console her, as he is consoled.

Left to Felipe and Sister Perpetua, Lena suspects, a minor legend of Theo's death, an edited version (concerning someone Lena no longer recognizes) might be shaped, the rough places smoothed away. And it might start with Felipe's report of "Not one stone!"

The coffin gleams from the depths.

Father Kamin ends with a promise: "Rest, pardon, and peace. . . . He has entered into peace. Deep peace." *Amen to that,* Lena breathes, eyeing the deep pit, her glance darting, slanting towards it and away, to the verge, and away. *Amen: may it be so.*

This book was set in Adobe Caslon Pro, designed by
Carol Twombly and released in 1990. The typeface is
named after the British typefounder William Caslon
(1692–1766) and grew out of Twombly's study of
Caslon's specimen sheets produced between 1734 and
1770. Though Caslon began his career making "exotic"
typefaces—Hebrew, Arabic, and Coptic—his Roman
typeface became the standard for text printed in English for most of the eighteenth century, including the
Declaration of Independence.

This book was designed by Shannon Carter,
Ian Creeger, and Gregory Wolfe. It was published in
hardcover, paperback, and electronic formats
by Wipf and Stock Publishers, Eugene, Oregon.

Made in the USA
Monee, IL
10 February 2021

60214199R00083